MW01235501

PRO SE ⚖ PRESS

THE GUNSMITH #400: THE LINCOLN RANSOM
A Pro Se Press Publication

The Lincoln Ransom is a work of historical fiction. Many of the important historical events, figures, and locations are as accurately portrayed as possible. In keeping with a work of fiction, various events and occurrences were invented by the author.

Edited by Tommy Hancock
Editor in Chief, Pro Se Productions—Tommy Hancock
Submissions Editor—Rachel Lampi
Director of Corporate Operations—Kristi King-Morgan
Publisher & Pro Se Productions, LLC-Chief Executive Officer—Fuller Bumpers

Cover Art by Jeffrey Hayes
Print Production and Book Design by Percival Constantine
New Pulp Logo Design by Sean E. Ali
New Pulp Seal Design by Cari Reese

Pro Se Productions, LLC
133 1/2 Broad Street
Batesville, AR, 72501
870-834-4022

editorinchief@prose-press.com
www.prose-press.com

Published in digital form by Piccadilly Publishing, April 2015

THE GUNSMITH

#400 THE LINCOLN RANSOM

J.R. ROBERTS

PRO SE PRESS

ONE

Denver, Colorado

When Clint entered the Denver House Hotel, it was almost like coming home he had been there so many times before.

The desk clerk looked up and recognized him as he approached the desk.

"Mr. Adams," the young man said. "How nice to have you back with us."

"Happy to be back," Clint said. He didn't remember the man's name at the moment. "Can I have a nice room?"

"Best room in the house, sir," the clerk said. "Those are our instructions whenever you come to town."

"That's nice to know."

Clint signed the register, accepted his key, and carried his saddlebags up the staircase to the second floor. The last time he was there, there was some talk of modernizing the hotel by installing an elevator, but it looked as if nothing like that had started yet.

When he got to his room, a two-room suite with its own water closet, he tossed the saddlebags on the bed and walked to the window. It was still light out, there was still traffic on the street below. Normally, Clint loved coming to Denver. He gambled, he ate at good restaurants, spent time with beautiful women, and had dinner with his friend, Talbot Roper. This trip it looked like he was only going to have time to see Roper.

But he was hungry and wanted a drink. He went into the WC washed off the remnants of the train trip from Washington to Springfield to Denver, then put on some clean clothes and went out.

The Denver House had its own excellent dining room that specialized in steaks and catered not only to guests, but to locals—a lot of businessmen, politicians, and citizens with enough money to pay the exorbitant prices.

He entered and was shown to a table that was against a wall and away from the doors and windows. He ordered a 16-ounce steak with everything and a mug of beer. He was finished with the beer by the time the steak came and asked for another.

While he ate he watched the people around him, tables of mostly twos and threes. They came, ate, and went while he enjoyed his meal slowly, and nobody seemed to be paying any special attention to him. Which suited him just fine.

Denver was a detour. People in Washington knew he was going to Springfield, but they didn't know where he was going after that. Actually, he didn't know he was going to go to Denver, either. Not until he decided he needed help on this. And that the help he got should not be connected to the United States Government. It should be someone he could trust without question.

That was Talbot Roper, possibly the best private detective in the country. He had a dinner appointment with Roper that evening, when he'd probably have another steak just like this one.

He signed the check so that the total would be added to his hotel bill when he checked out, then left the hotel to go for a walk. A few blocks west he found a small saloon he'd been to once or twice before and went inside. It was about half full of locals, who only glanced at him when he entered. He went to the bar and ordered a beer.

He thought about Eclipse. He had brought the Darley Arabian with him, taken him off the train, and installed him at a livery stable near the train station. He didn't know if he'd be leaving Denver by train or on horseback. That would depend on what—if anything—he learned while he was there.

He nursed his beer and checked the time. Still several hours before he had to meet Roper in the lobby of the Denver House. Roper, as qualified as he was, had actually been Clint's third choice for someone to ask help from. First he had tried places he thought the man might be, but he hadn't been able to locate him. Then there was his friend Rick Hartman, from Labyrinth, Texas. Hartman had contacts all over the country, but he rarely, if ever, left Labyrinth. That left Talbot Roper. It had only taken one telegram to set up a meeting with his friend.

He hadn't told Roper anything about why he was coming, only that he was, and that he needed his help. That was enough for Roper to drop what he was doing and agree to meet with Clint.

He finished his beer, left the saloon and headed back to the Denver House.

***

As he entered the hotel the desk clerk waved him over.

"I have a message for you, Mr. Adams," he said, handing him a slip of paper.

"Who left it?"

"A young boy."

"Thanks."

Clint looked around the lobby, saw nothing suspicious, took the note up to his room with him before reading it.

It was from Roper. It said: "Something's come up. Let's meet at 9 a.m. for breakfast." It was signed "Roper."

Clint read some Mark Twain the rest of the evening, and went to bed.

TWO

lint was in the lobby the next morning when Talbot Roper came walking in at eight-fifty-five a.m. He saw Clint and walked toward him with his hand out. The two men shook hands warmly.

"Good to see you, Clint," Roper said.

"Thanks for coming."

"Sorry about last night," the detective said. "Just had to tie up some old business. Shall we have breakfast?"

"By all means. I skipped dinner last night, fell asleep early. Train rides, you know?"

"I know," Roper said. "They're taking more and more out of me, too. Rather ride a horse anytime."

They walked to the dining room, which was only about half full at that time of the morning. Clint had them taken to the same table he'd had the evening before. They both ordered steak-and-eggs and coffee.

"Well," Roper said, "I'm all yours, Clint. My slate is clean."

"I have a story to tell you," Clint said. "Started almost a week ago."

"By all means," Roper said, "tell me a story, Clint..."

***

Labyrinth, Texas

Clint was in Labyrinth, Texas when he got the tele-gram to come to Washington D.C..

"Jim West?" Rick Hartman asked.

"No," Clint said, "but close. Jeremy Pike."

"The Government?"

Clint nodded, folding the telegram. It was morning and they were sitting in Rick's Place, a saloon and gam-bling hall that was not open yet.

"Yes."

"And when the government calls you always go run-ning, don't you?"

Clint shrugged. "I'm a patriot."

"Yeah, I'm a patriot, too," Rick said, "but that just means I vote. What do they want you to do this time?"

"I won't know that until I get there," Clint said, as Rick's bartender brought their breakfasts out.

Rick shook his head. "You know, I'm glad I don't leave town anymore."

"I think it's a condition with you now," Clint said. "I don't think you could leave if you wanted to."

Rick smiled and cut off a hunk of ham steak.

"Then it's lucky I don't want to."

***

Each trip back to Labyrinth Clint would meet a new group of girls working for Rick in his saloon. Saloon girls did not stick around for very long, looking for any reason to move on to the next town, the next job. But Rick had a system. He usually hired one older woman—early thirties, maybe—and then the rest all under thirty, and the older woman became like a den mother to the others.

And Rick had extremely good taste in women. The

girls were always beautiful. And he usually picked out a young one for himself.

The last few years, though, Clint had found himself spending time with the "den mother."

Elizabeth Downing was 33, and while that may have seemed old for a saloon girl, there was nothing over-the-hill about Liz. She was a busty blonde whose breasts were still high and firm, and who was still slim-waisted, appearing even moreso because of her hourglass hips.

He had been in Labyrinth for several weeks when the telegram came—a longer stay than usual. But he had spent a lot of time on the trail recently, and a good long rest in Labyrinth had been just what he needed—and so had Liz.

They were in bed together the night he received the telegram, and he told her he'd be leaving the next morning.

"That's kind of abrupt, isn't it?" she asked. She propped herself up on an elbow, her long blonde hair flowing down over her shoulders. One large breast was flattened beneath her, but he could see the large, pink nipple of the other one very clearly.

"It can't be helped," he said. "My country calls."

"Your country, huh?" she said. "Not another woman?"

"Definitely not another woman," he said, reaching out to cup her breast and thumb her nipple. She closed her eyes and bit her lush lower lip.

"You bastard," she said, "you know I may not be here when you get back."

"I have no idea when I'll be back," he said, "or if."

"Oh, Mr. Adams," she said, lifting his hand to her mouth, running the tip of his thumb over her bottom lip, "you're a bad risk for any woman, aren't you? She'd never know if you were alive or dead."

He pushed his thumb between her lips into her mouth, and she sucked on it.

"I'm afraid that's always going to be the case, Liz."

She sucked his thumb until it was thoroughly wet, and then he slid it from her mouth and circled her nipple with it again.

"Oh, God..." she said.

She pushed him down onto his back, kissed his mouth hungrily, then kissed his chest and his belly, running her tongue around his navel, and then lower still. When she was nestled comfortably between his legs, her elbows resting on his thighs, she licked the head of his penis and then drew it into her mouth. She sucked it a while, just the spongy head, getting it very wet, holding his thick penis with one hand. Then, little by little, she took more of it into her mouth, until suddenly she swooped down on him, causing him to catch his breath.

She began to suck him with long, slow strokes of her lips and tongue, holding onto the base of his penis with one hand, using the other hand to cup and caress his swollen testicles.

She allowed his cock to slide out of her mouth and looked up at him with her beautiful blue eyes. "You're gonna miss me, aren't you?"

"Terribly."

She stroked his cock with her hand and said, "How much?"

"Awfully," he said, "thoroughly... amazingly... what else do you want me to say?"

"Nothing," she said. "You've said enough. Here's your reward."

She took him into her hot, hungry mouth again and sucked him until he lifted his hips off the bed, bellowed, and exploded into her mouth...

THREE

Washington, D.C.

Clint took the train to Washington D.C., taking Eclipse with him in the stock car every step of the way. Since there was no telling what they wanted with him this time, he didn't know whether or not he'd need the horse.

In Washington he walked the Darley Arabian off the train and put him in a livery stable nearby, one that he had used before on other trips.

"I may need him at a moment's notice," he told the hostler.

"He'll be ready," the man said. "God, I've never seen a horse like this. Is he fast?"

"Fast," Clint said, "and he can run all day."

The man stroked Eclipse's neck, which Clint found encouraging. The horse didn't let a lot of people touch him. He must have sensed this man knew what he was doing.

Clint also left his saddle in the livery, but took his rifle and saddlebags with him. He went back to the train station, where he found a carriage waiting for him.

"Mr. Adams?" the driver asked.

"That's right."

"I've been sent to pick you up, sir."

"Fine." He tossed his saddlebags into the carriage.

"Are we going to a hotel?"

"No, sir," the man said. "They're very anxious to see you. I'm to take you to meet with them."

"With who?"

"I'm not at liberty to say, sir."

"Okay, then," Clint said. "That sounds pretty standard for the government."

"Yes, sir."

"Okay, then," Clint said, climbing aboard. "Let's go."

***

When the carriage pulled up in front of a concrete stairway that led up to a large building, Jeremy Pike was waiting there.

"Clint," Pike said as Clint stepped down. "Good to see you." They shook hands.

"What's going on, Jeremy?"

"I was just asked to meet you and take you up."

"Up there?" Clint asked, pointing to the building.

"Yes."

"What is this place?"

"A botanical garden."

"A wha—you're going to show me flowers?"

"Clint," Pike said, "somebody wants to talk to you. This is serious."

"Yeah, okay," Clint said. "Lead the way."

***

The building was, indeed, a botanical garden. Pike took Clint down along rows and rows of flowers until they reached the far end of the building. Standing in front of a window were two men, one of them in uniform.

They were staring out the window—the view was of the Potomac River.

When they reached the two men they turned to face them.

"Clint Adams, this is Mr. Henry Goulding of the State Department, and General George Wilson."

"Mr. Adams," Goulding said, "it's a pleasure to meet you. Thank you for coming."

"Mr. Adams," the General said, also shaking hands.

"Sir," Clint said.

"Pike," Goulding said, "I'd like you to stay."

"Yes, sir."

"All right, gentlemen," Clint asked, "are we all here?"

"We are," Goulding said.

"I don't suppose there's someplace we can sit?" Clint said. "Those were a lot of stairs."

"Afraid not," the General said. "This meeting is top secret."

"All right, then," Clint said, folding his arms.

"You plan on wearing that gun everywhere you go in D.C.?" the General asked.

"You betcha," Clint said. "I don't wear a gun, I'm dead."

"We can provide protection—"

"Never mind that," Clint said. "I provide my own protection. Can we get to the top secret part?"

The General looked at Goulding, who stepped forward to take the lead.

"Let's walk, Mr. Adams."

Clint looked at the General, who gestured that he should go ahead. Goulding started to walk and Clint fell into step next to him. They walked along the rows of flowers.

"Why do I get the feeling you somehow outrank a General?" Clint asked.

"Just on this thing, Mr. Adams."

"And this thing is... what?"

"Something where we need someone we can trust," Goulding said.

"You have thousands of soldiers, and I don't know how many secret service agents."

"We need someone who is not in the military and not in the government. You were recommended by several people."

"Jim West?"

"Among them, yes," Goulding said. "Also Mr. Pike."

"All right, then," Clint said. "What exactly are we talking about?"

By now they had left the General and Pike behind, out of earshot. Clint didn't know if that had been the point of walking.

"It's a ransom situation."

"Ah... a big ransom?"

"Very big."

"So somebody important has been kidnapped?"

"Yes."

"And you've already heard from the kidnappers?" Clint asked.

"We have, yes."

"Where do they want the payoff made?"

"Colorado."

"What? Why Colorado?"

"We don't know. It's a long way from where the kidnapping took place. We don't understand it."

"But somebody here in D.C. has been contacting you with their demands."

"Yes."

"Seems to me you need to find whoever that is, here in D.C.," Clint said. "Why send anybody to Colorado?"

"We have somebody working on it at this end," Goulding said.

"Pike?"

"Yes."

"Okay, so while he works on it here you want me to take the ransom to Colorado."

"That's right."

"Where in Colorado?"

"A town called Segundo. Do you know it?"

"Yes. It's a small town south of Trinidad, just this side of the New Mexico border."

"See?" Goulding said. "Already you're paying dividends. You know the area."

"How much money am I going to be carrying?"

"I need you to agree before I tell you."

"Then I need you to tell me who's been kidnapped before I agree. I assume you're expecting me to bring the victim back alive?"

'Well, not exactly."

"What do you mean?"

"The victim... well, the victim's name is Lincoln."

"Lincoln?" Clint asked. "As in Abraham Lincoln?"

"Yes."

"Okay, which one?" Clint asked. "His wife, one of his kids—"

"No," Goulding said, "I said Abraham Lincoln."

Clint stared at him.

"Are you telling me that Abraham Lincoln has been kidnapped?"

"What I'm telling you is," Goulding said, "Abraham Lincoln's corpse has been stolen."

FOUR

"**O**kay, let me get this straight," Clint said. He stopped walking and turned to face Goulding, who also stopped. "Somebody has snatched Abraham Lincoln's body from his Tomb in Springfield, Illinois, and is offering to ransom it back to the United States Government?"

"You've got it."

"For how much?"

"A hundred thousand dollars."

"And you want me to pay them?"

"We do."

"And retrieve the body."

"Yes."

"Wow."

They stood there for a few seconds while Clint digested the information.

"When was the body taken?"

"We're not sure," Goulding said. "Apparently it was removed without us knowing about it. When we were contacted we naturally dispatched someone to determine if it was true."

"And it was."

"Yes."

"So how long have you known?"

"About three weeks. It took us a week to get you

here."

"So you don't even know exactly when it was removed?"

"No."

"And when is the ransom scheduled to be paid?"

"We know the place, but not the time. We'll have to stay in touch by telegram."

Clint jerked his chin toward the river.

"Do they know about this? The General and Pike?"

"They know about a kidnapping and a ransom," Goulding said. "The fact that it is Abraham Lincoln's body is on a need-to-know basis."

"And they don't need to know?"

"Not at the moment."

"And who knows besides you and me?" Clint asked.

"People at the cemetery in Springfield," Goulding said, "but that's being handled."

"And nobody else in D.C.?"

"The President."

"And does he know you're calling me in?"

"Yes," Goulding said. "In fact, he approved you, personally."

"Why don't you hire a detective, Mr. Goulding?" Clint asked. "I can recommend a very good one."

"If you want to bring somebody in to work with you on this," Goulding said, "and you vouch for them, then go ahead. But we want you."

They started walking again.

"Did somebody really get Lincoln's body out of his tomb?" he asked.

"Out of his tomb, out of the cemetery, apparently out of Springfield."

"And my directive is..."

"...pay the ransom, get the body back."

16

"Which one takes precedence?"

"Getting the body back."

"If I agree to do this," Clint said, "I'll want to do it my way."

"Of course," Goulding said. "If you take the assignment, you'll be given your head to do as you see fit."

"So you won't have a problem if I want to stop in Springfield on my way back West?"

"Why?"

"It's how I want to start."

Goulding shrugged. "All right, fine. I'll leave word you're to have the run of the place."

"Good."

"So you'll take the assignment?"

"Expenses?"

"You'll be given an appropriate war chest," Goulding said, "and a bonus when you get the job done."

"I'm not worried about a bonus for doing my country a service, Mr. Goulding."

"Nevertheless," Goulding said, "the bonus will be there."

They were walking up a row, heading back to where Pike and the General were standing, staring out at the river and talking.

"You're not going to want Pike on this, are you?" Goulding asked.

"No," Clint said. "I already have someone in mind. Besides, you have him working on this end, right?"

"That's right."

"Okay, then," Clint said. "Is there anything else you have to tell me?"

"I don't think so."

"What about the Lincoln family?"

"What about them?"

"What do they know?"

"Nothing," Goulding said. "We want to get the body back without them ever having been aware it was gone."

"You want it back before anyone in the country knows it's gone."

"That's correct."

"I assume you have me checked into a hotel?"

"You have a suite at the Sumner House. The bar and the restaurant will be covered."

"One night?"

"I assumed you'd want to get started right away."

"I do."

"Your driver will take you there. Did you bring your horse?"

"I did. He's in a livery near the station. I'll be taking him back with me."

"Just let us know what the bill is."

"I can handle that myself," Clint said.

They reached Pike and the General, who both turned and stared at them expectantly.

"Mr. Adams is on board."

"Excellent!" the General said.

"I'll get started tomorrow," Clint said.

"Mr. Pike, will you take Mr. Adams back to his carriage?" Goulding asked.

"Of course."

"Mr. Adams," Goulding said, extending his hand, "I'm looking forward to hearing from you."

"I'll need a little more information."

"There will be a file in your hotel room," Goulding assured him, "with all the information you need."

"Thank you."

"This way," Pike said.

As they headed down the rows of flowers leaving

Goulding and the General behind, Pike said, "I don't suppose you can let me know what's going on?"

"It's on a need-to-know basis, Jeremy."

Pike nodded. "I know all about that."

He walked him back down the stone staircase to where the carriage was waiting. The two men shook hands.

"I'll handle my end," Pike said, "even though I'm in the dark."

"I know I can count on you," Clint said.

He climbed into the carriage and waved at Pike as the driver pulled away.

FIVE

Denver, Colorado

"Wait a minute," Roper said, looking around. They had finished their breakfast, and so had everyone else. The other tables were mostly empty, while they had another pot of coffee between them. "Let me get this straight."

"I know," Clint said. "That's what I kept thinking."

"Somebody got into the cemetery in Springfield, into the Lincoln Tomb, and got away with the body of President Lincoln?"

"That's the story."

"And you believe it?"

"Why else would they send me out here with a hundred thousand dollars?"

"Where's the money?"

"I can get to it when I need it," Clint said.

"Okay, I get it," Roper said. "Need to know." Roper poured them each another cup of coffee. "So I guess you went to Springfield?"

"I went."

"So there's more to the story."

"Lots more."

Roper looked around.

"Well, this place will stay empty 'til lunch time,"

Roper said. "It's as good a place as any to hear the rest."

***

Springfield, Illinois

Clint had been to Springfield before, but not for some time. Certainly not since President Lincoln had been buried.

He took Eclipse off the stock car and walked the horse into town. Last time there he'd stayed at a place called The Walnut Inn. When he got to Walnut Street he saw that the hotel was still there, and there was a livery stable across the street.

"You stayin' at the Inn?" the hostler asked.

"I will be when I check in," Clint said. "Why?"

"You get a cheaper rate if you stay there."

"Well, I'm going over there to check in right now."

"Just tell the gal at the desk Rufus sent ya over. Sure is a right fine lookin' animal," the old man said. "Best I ever seen, and I been doin' this job for a long time."

"Just take good care of him," Clint said.

"You can count on it."

Clint took his rifle and saddlebags and crossed the street to the Inn. Behind the counter a pretty girl watched as he approached.

"Help ya?" she asked.

"I'd like a room."

"For how long?"

"A day or two."

"Did you put your horse in the livery across the street?" she asked.

"I sure did," Clint said. "Rufus told me to mention him."

"Okay, then," she said, turning the register toward him. "Sign in please."

He signed his real name.

"Clint Adams?" she asked.

"That's right."

"The Gunsmith?"

"Right again."

"Well," she said, "what brings you to Springfield?"

"I heard they had real pretty girls here," he answered. "I can see they were right."

"Oh..." she said, blushing.

"Also, I thought I'd take a look at Lincoln's Tomb."

"We're right proud to have the President buried here, where he practiced law."

"I'm sure you are," Clint said. "My key?'

"Oh, sure. Sorry." She handed him a key. "Second floor."

"Thanks."

As he started for the stairs she said, "My name's Angie, if you need anything."

He smiled and asked, "What's your name if I don't need anything."

"Aww..." she said.

***

Up in his room he found a sturdy bed big enough for one person, a chest of drawers with a pitcher and bowl on it, and one chair. It looked just the way the room looked last time he was there, except it was cleaner. That time there had been an old man behind the desk, sleeping. Apparently, the place was owned by new folks who kept it clean.

He washed his hands and face in the pitcher, then put

his hat back on and went out to find a meal. It was late afternoon, so he wouldn't be going to the cemetery until morning.

Down in the lobby the girl stood up straight when he came down. She looked as if she had just combed her hair. Her simple cotton dress clung to her solid young body.

"Where can I get a good steak, Angie?" he asked.

"Just down the street, Mr. Adams. Place called Frieda's. Tell 'em I sent you, they'll give ya a break on the price."

"Sounds like you folks in Springfield work together to make your guests feel real welcome."

"We try."

"I'll see you later."

SIX

He found Frieda's with no problem, a small café that was doing a fine business this time of the afternoon. He only hoped there was a table for him.

He went inside and could tell by the smells that Frieda knew her business.

A man with a white shirt and black tie approached him and said, "Table, sir?"

"If you've got one."

"Oh, yes, sir," the man said, "but it's in the back. Is that all right?"

"That's my favorite place," Clint said.

"This way."

The other diners watched as he followed the waiter across the room.

"I'm staying at the Walnut Inn," Clint told the man. "Angie told me to mention that."

"Angie's a nice girl," the man said. "What can I get you, sir?"

"A nice thick fat steak with all the trimmings."

"That's our specialty, sir. And to drink?"

"Coffee," Clint said. "Nice and strong."

"Comin' up."

The coffee was just the way he liked it, as was the steak. He ate with great pleasure, watching the people around him, as he always did, looking for someone showing undue or unwanted interest in him. But the people in Frieda's seemed to only be interested in the people they were dining with.

When he was finished the waiter brought his bill, which he would have gladly paid in full if they weren't giving him a break for staying at the Inn.

"Come back, sir," the waiter said. "If you're still in town, that is."

"I'll be here a day or two," Clint said. "Tell Frieda it was a great steak."

"Frieda was my wife," the man said. "She died several years ago. I keep the café going in her name."

"I'm sorry. The food is very good."

"I make everything to her recipes," he said. "My name is Arthur Blair."

"Clint," Clint said, shaking the man's hand. "I'll be back for breakfast."

He walked back to the hotel, but instead of going inside he used a chair out front to sit a while.

After about twenty minutes of him watching the occasional person or buggy or wagon go by, Angie came out the door and leaned against the building.

"What are you looking at?" she asked. She was still wearing the simple cotton dress, but smelled as if she had applied a fresh scent to her hair or skin.

"Just watching," he said.

"Is that what you came here to do?" she asked. "Watch?"

"No," he said. "Tomorrow I'm going to Lincoln's Tomb, but tonight I thought I'd just relax and watch the town go by."

"Well," she said, "ain't much of it goes by here."

"I noticed," he said. "Just an occasional wagon."

"Most of the traffic is over on Sangamon Street."

"Where's the cemetery from here?"

"Not far," she said. "It's over on Monument Avenue. It's called the Oak Ridge Cemetery."

"Can I walk from here, or should I take my horse?" he asked.

"You can walk," she said. "In fact, if you like, I can walk you over there."

"I wouldn't want to take you away from your work," he said. "Maybe get you fired."

"I doubt my dad would fire me," she said.

"Your family owns the hotel?"

"Yes," she said. "In fact, I was only behind the desk because the regular girl went home sick. She should be back tomorrow and I'll be able to walk you there."

"Well, all right," he said.

"What time would you like to go?" she asked.

"Well, I told Arthur I'd come by for breakfast," he said. "Can I take you to breakfast first?"

"Why, yes, sir, you may," she said. "What time?"

"I'll stop by the front desk and pick you up at eight a.m.."

"Perfect," she said. "I'll see you in the morning."

"You'll see me when I come back inside to go to my room," he pointed out.

"No, I'm finished for the day. I'm going home. My father will be behind the desk."

"Oh," he said. "Okay, until tomorrow, then."

"Goodnight."

She went inside, presumably to say goodnight to her father, and then apparently left by another door.

He remained outside until it was full dark and traffic had stopped completely. When there was nothing left to see he stood and went into the lobby.

The man behind the desk looked up from what he

was writing and watched Clint approach. He was a short man in his fifties, with a ring of fuzz around a bald head.

"Mr. Adams?"

"That's right."

"Angie told me you were out there," he said. "My name's Ben. I own the hotel."

"Nice to meet you." Clint stepped up and shook the man's hand.

"I understand you're in town to see Lincoln's Tomb," Ben said.

"Yes, sir, that's right."

"Well," Ben said, "enjoy your stay."

"I'm sure I will."

Clint went up the stairs, wondering if Angie had told her father she was going to be Clint's guide in the morning. He did not get a very friendly feeling from the man.

SEVEN

Clint woke the next morning early, feeling rested. He used the pitcher and basin to wash, put on a clean shirt, and went down to the lobby where Angie was waiting. She was wearing another cotton dress, but this one much brighter and prettier, with a bit of a scooped neck that showed some pale, smooth skin. She'd seemed very young when he first checked in, but now he judged her to be about twenty-five.

"Good morning," she said.

"'Morning," he replied. "You look lovely this morning."

"Thank you." She blushed.

Behind the desk was a woman in her thirties, rather plain and shapeless.

"This is Kathy," Angie said. "She wasn't feeling too well yesterday, but she's better today."

"I'm pregnant," Kathy said.

"Congratulations," Clint said.

"Come on," Angie said, slipping her arm into his. "I'm hungry."

They went out the front door.

* * *

They chatted on the way to Frieda's, Angie explain-

THE GUNSMITH #400 - THE LINCOLN RANSOM

ing how the woman had died from what had looked like a slight case of measles.

"Did she infect anyone else?" he asked.

"No," Angie said, "that's what was amazing. It was only her. She had so many friends, and we all mourned her loss. Arthur's been keeping the café going."

When they got to the café only a few of the tables were taken. Arthur was very happy to see Angie, and Clint as well. He showed them to a table and brought them coffee.

"Steak-and-eggs," Clint said.

"Ham-and-eggs, Arthur," Angie said.

"Comin' up," he said, happily.

While Clint and Angie ate people began to stream in for breakfast, and by eight-forty-five the place was full.

Angie asked him many questions about himself, his reputation, his adventures, all of which he skirted.

"You know," he said to her at one point, "I don't give out interviews to newspaper people."

"I don't work for a newspaper."

"But you are interviewing me," he said. "Or interrogating me."

"I'm sorry," she said. "I've never been anywhere but here. I'm curious."

"You'll have to start travelling, Angie," he said. "You can get to Chicago from here very easily."

"I know!" she said, her eyes wide. "I'm planning to go, but I'm saving money for the trip."

"It's something to look forward to," Clint said. "You'll love Chicago."

They continued talking and eating until Angie said it was time to go.

***

30

Angie walked him over to Monument Avenue and the entrance to the Oak Ridge Cemetery. It was a huge expanse of rolling fields and headstones and markers of different sizes and shapes.

She walked him to the entrance of the tomb, but when he tried the doors, they were locked.

"Let's go to the office," he said.

"It's not usually locked," she said, confused.

"Well, maybe it's just not open yet."

They walked over to the cemetery office, which was open at that time of the morning.

"I'll just talk to the manager," Clint said. "Why don't you sit here?"

There was a bench that Angie could sit on and Clint left her there and went to the counter, where a man in a suit stood, staring at him expectantly.

"Yes, sir?"

"I'd like to see the manager."

"And what is this about, sir?"

"Just tell him that Clint Adams is here to see him," Clint said. "He'll understand."

"Adams?"

"That's right."

"Do you wish to inter—"

"Just tell him."

The man blinked, then said, "Uh, well, yes, sir. If you'll wait right here, please."

The man left the desk and went through a door into the back of the building somewhere. There were some muffled voices, nothing he could understand, and then suddenly the man reappeared, followed by a second man, also in a suit. The second man was taller, older, and looked to be in charge.

"Mr. Adams?" he asked.

"That's right."

"My name is Harold Glanville, sir," he said. "I manage the Oak Ridge Cemetery. Would you come to my office, please?"

"Sure."

He turned and held up one finger to Angie, then followed the man.

In a small office the man turned and extended his hand.

"I'm so glad you're here," he said, as they shook. "I was told to extend you every cooperation."

"Well, you can start by unlocking the tomb. Have you been keeping it locked since the... incident?"

"Oh, no!" he said, eyes wide. "We couldn't do that. It would start tongues wagging."

"Yes, it would. Can we go over there now and unlock it? I'd like to get a look inside."

"Yes, of course," Glanville said. "Let me get the keys."

"I have someone with me," Clint said. "She lives here and brought me over here. I'll go out and wait with her."

"What does she know?" the man asked anxiously.

"Nothing. What do you have in the tomb at the moment?"

"There's a coffin in there," Glanville said. "An empty casket."

"All right," Clint said. "I'll wait outside."

"I'll be right there."

He went out to where Angie was waiting.

"What's going on?" she asked.

"The manager is going to unlock the tomb for us."

"Wow," she said, "did you tell him who you are?"

"Well, yeah."

She stood up and smiled.

32

"I guess you get a lot of things done that way, don't you?" she asked.

He decided to go ahead and let her think he was throwing his weight around.

"Sometimes."

Glanville came out and Clint introduced him to Angie. The three of them walked through the cemetery to the tomb, Glanville chattering about the history of the place and some of the famous people who were interred there. Clint could hear how nervous the man was.

When they reached the tomb the manager used the keys to open the heavy metal doors.

"Just let me go inside and light the interior."

They waited while he went inside, and then returned.

"Shall I take you inside?" he asked.

"No, that's all right," Clint said. "We'll have a look around. You're going to keep the doors unlocked anyway, right? For the rest of the day?"

"That's correct."

"I'll come and let you know when we're done."

"I'd appreciate that, sir."

The manager walked away, very reluctantly.

"Should we go inside?"

EIGHT

The inside was dimly lit by torches. They made their way through the tomb toward the casket, which—as far as Angie was concerned—contained the body of the deceased President Abraham Lincoln.

"Well," Angie said, "there he is."

But Clint wasn't interested in what he knew was an empty casket. He was looking around at the interior of the tomb, wondering how someone had gotten in and gotten out with the President's casket.

"What are you looking at?" she asked.

"Everything," he said. "I'll never have a tomb like this when I'm gone. I'm wondering how secure it is."

"Well, it's got those metal doors," she said. "That seems pretty secure. How could anybody get in here?"

"I don't know," Clint said, looking around. To appease her he spent some time staring at the casket.

"Did you ever meet President Lincoln?" she asked.

"I did," he said. "Several times."

"Would you eat supper with me tonight and tell me about it?"

"Sure," he said. "Listen, since I knew the President, would you go outside and give me a few minutes alone?"

"Of course," she said. "I'll be right outside."

As Angie left Clint began to walk around the tomb, checking the walls and the floors. He walked to just inside the metal doors and inspected them. They were large, solid doors, but they had a lock. Any door with a lock can be opened. They must have come in that way, right through the front doors.

He stepped outside to find Angie waiting with her hands behind her back.

"Angie, why don't you go back to work?" he said. "I've got to go and talk to the manager again."

"What about?"

"Just something that occurred to me while I was inside," he said. "I appreciate you showing me the way over here, but I can find my way back."

'Well, all right," she said. "I do have to get to work. But you're gonna tell me about you and Mr. Lincoln, remember?"

"Í remember."

They walked as far as the office together, and then she continued on out the gates.

The clerk behind the counter looked startled when Clint entered again.

"Sir?"

"I'd like to see Mr. Glanville again," he said. "I told him I'd let him know when I was done."

"Y-yessir."

The clerk took Clint back to the office. When Glanville saw him he rose from behind his desk.

"Can I help you with something else?" he asked.

"Just some questions."

"Please, have a seat."

Clint sat across from him.

"Can I offer you anything?"

"No, I'm fine. From what I can see of the tomb it's pretty secure."

"So we thought," Glanville said. "We were very

proud of it."

"I'm thinking whoever stole the casket must have come in right through the front doors," Clint said. "Somehow they got the lock open."

"That's what we figured."

"Do you have a head of security?"

"We do."

"I'd like to talk to him."

"I can arrange that," Glanville said. "Can you come back later?"

"Just say when."

"This afternoon, at four," the manager said. "He'll be available to you."

"What's his name?"

"Brad Wyatt."

"Does he know the President is missing?"

"Yes."

"Who else knows?"

"Brad and I," Glanville said. "We've kept it from the other employees."

"What do they think happened?"

"Only that the tomb was broken into," Glanville said, "that someone attempted to vandalize it."

"Tell me," Clint said, "why didn't you notify the government right away?"

"We, uh, thought we'd get a ransom demand and be able to handle it ourselves."

"But you didn't."

"No."

"How long did you wait?"

"A week," Glanville said, "uh, maybe longer."

"Okay," Clint said, standing. "I'll be here at four."

The two men shook hands, and then Clint Adams left.

***

After Adams was gone Glanville sat behind his desk for a while, then went out to the front.

"David," he said to the clerk.

"Yessir?"

"Find Brad Wyatt for me."

"He'll be here in a couple of hours, sir."

"Well," Glanville said, "I want to see him before that. Find him for me... now!"

"Yessir," David said. "Whatever you say."

Glanville went back into his office, closed the door, went to a small portable bar he had against the wall, and poured himself a stiff brandy.

It was only the first one he thought he was going to be needing.

NINE

lint did not go right back to the hotel.

Instead, he walked around Springfield, thinking what he was thinking when he was inside the tomb. What if this was an inside job? That was why he wanted to talk to the head of security, Brad Wyatt.

But there was somebody else he should be talking to, but he didn't know if the local police were aware of what happened.

In Washington he'd been given a file in his hotel room to read, had all the facts of the theft they were aware of—which wasn't much. Still, he'd been told to destroy the file before he left D.C.

The other thing they had given him was a special telegraph address he could use to get in touch with them, give them information, or ask them a question.

He found the Springfield telegraph office and wrote out a telegram, worded carefully.

THINKING OF TALKING TO LOCAL POLICE. WHAT DO YOU THINK. STOP. C.A.

The reply was almost immediate.

NO!

So, no police. The locals had no idea that Lincoln's body was not in the tomb.

On the other hand the police must have heard the same story that Glanville told his employees, that the tomb was vandalized.

He decided to talk to them anyway, without sending another telegram to D.C..

He left the telegraph office after getting directions to the police department.

***

The police department was a two-story building on Chestnut Street. As he entered he saw what had become a familiar sight in these eastern style police stations, the front desk. As he approached, the sergeant manning the desk did not look up, but spoke.

"Can I help you?"

"Yes," Clint said, "I'd like to talk to whoever is in charge of the case of vandalism at the President's Tomb in Oak Ridge Cemetery."

The sergeant looked up this time. He was a big man in his late forties, with creases in his face. And he needed a shave.

"The President's Tomb?"

"Yes," Clint said. "Lincoln."

The sergeant leaned his elbows on the desk.

"Do you have information about who might have done it?" the man asked.

"Let's say I have an interest."

"Why should anybody talk to you?"

"Why not let the officer or detective in charge make that decision?"

The sergeant studied Clint for a few moments, then looked down at the gun on his hip.

"We don't allow guns, you know."

"I'm a special case."

"Oh yeah? Why's that?"

40

"Because if I take off my gun," Clint said, "I'm dead."

"How's that?"

"You're not asking the right question, Sergeant."

"All right," the man said, standing upright and folding his arms, "what's your name?"

"There you go," Clint said. "My name is Clint Adams."

If the policeman didn't recognize the name, then maybe Clint was out of luck. But he could see from the look on the man's face that wasn't the case.

"The Gunsmith," the sergeant said. It wasn't a question, so Clint said nothing. "Wait here."

The sergeant left the desk and when into the bowels of the building, came back with a man following him. Thus one was in his thirties, wearing a gray three-piece suit with a watch chain hanging from the vest.

"Sergeant Webber tells me you're interested in the vandalism of President Lincoln's Tomb."

"I am."

"And that your name is Clint Adams."

"It is."

"And that makes you the Gunsmith."

"It does."

"Do you have anything on you that proves that?"

"No."

"Are you staying in Springfield?"

"Yes, I'm checked into the Walnut Inn."

"Anything in your room with your name on it?"

"Some letters, maybe. A book."

"A book?"

"I write my name in the inside cover of books I'm reading."

"Well," the man said, "we can go over to the Walnut

41

Inn and look into this later. Right now, my name is Detective Dan Kingman. Why don't you come back to my office with me and we'll talk about... things?"

"Lead the way, Detective."

Clint followed Kingman through the building until they reached a small office with a desk and two chairs.

"Have a seat, Mr. Adams," Kingman said, "and tell me what you're doing here."

TEN

"What brings you to Springfield?" Kingman asked. "Not the vandalism?"

"Well, no," Clint said. "I actually went to the cemetery this morning to see the tomb and heard about the vandalism. So, I thought I'd come here and see what you had."

"Why?"

"The truth is," Clint said, "I knew Lincoln, and I don't like the idea of anybody vandalizing his tomb."

"I see," Kingman said. "Well, the fact is they didn't do much. They got the front doors open, but must have gotten scared away before they could do much damage. At least, that's what Brad Wyatt had to say."

"Brad Wyatt?"

"The head of security at the cemetery."

"Ah."

"So if you're interested in knowing more," Kingman said, "maybe you should talk to him."

"Maybe I should," Clint said. "I'll stop by the cemetery again later."

"And if you find anything out," Kingman said, "anything helpful, maybe you could pass it on to me."

"I'll do that."

Clint stood up, then paused.

"You still want to come over to the Walnut Inn and

look at my room?"

"Later," Kingman said, "I'll do that later."

"Okay," Clint said. "See you then."

"You can find your own way out without getting lost?" Kingman asked.

"Sure," Clint said. "I dropped bread crumbs."

"What?"

"I'll be fine."

Clint left the office.

***

After Adams was gone Kingman left his office, walked to another part of the building, and knocked on a closed door.

"What?"

He opened it. A florid-faced man in his fifties sat behind a desk. The red face was one usually found on an overweight man, but this one was almost painfully thin. He was in shirt sleeves, the sleeves rolled up on his stick-like forearms, his jacket hanging on a coat rack by the door, along with his hat. He was staring down at papers on his desk while he spoke.

"Chief."

"Kingman." Chief Stevens said, "What can I do for you?"

"I just had an interesting visitor."

"Really?" He looked up at the detective. "You want to sit and tell me about it?"

"Yes, sir."

Stevens waved him to a chair and the detective sat.

"Who was your visitor?"

"Clint Adams."

The Chief didn't react.

"The Gunsmith?"

"I know who Clint Adams is," the Chief said. "What did he want?"

"He was interested in what happened at the cemetery."

"The vandalism of the President's Tomb?"

"Yes sir."

"You're still thinking about that, Dan?"

"I just think there's something else going on here, Chief," Kingman said. "Something other than simple vandalism."

"But Glanville and Wyatt both say there's nothing."

"I know," Kingman said, "but why would the Gunsmith be interested?"

"Why did he say he was interested?"

"He says he knew Lincoln personally."

"I'll bet he did," the Chief said. "Somebody like that would probably know a lot of famous people. However..."

"What?"

"Are you sure he really is Adams, the Gunsmith?"

"I'm going to go to his hotel and check, but yeah, I'm sure it's him."

"How can you be so sure?"

"Why would someone claim to be him," Kingman said, "and put a target like that on their back?"

"You have a point. Was he wearing a gun?"

"Yes, and he wouldn't take it off."

"Did you ask him to?"

"No, but the desk sergeant said he wouldn't take it off. He said if he removed it, he'd be dead."

"Sounds like something a gunfighter would say," the Chief said.

"Yeah, it does."

"What do you want to do, Dan?"

"Keep an eye on him," Kingman said, "see what he does."

"And if he leaves Springfield?"

Kingman shrugged. "That would be the end of it, then."

"All right," the Chief said. "See where it leads you."

"Thank you, sir."

"And keep me informed."

"Yessir." Kingman left the office.

ELEVEN

Clint still didn't go back to the hotel. He was afraid that Angie would distract him from what he had to do. It was too early in the day to be distracted. He walked around Springfield some more, admiring the way the city had grown since he'd last been there. Then he found a small café and went in to have lunch. He chose chicken because he didn't want to compare their steak to Frieda's.

After lunch he walked again. Returning to the hotel might not only distract him, but he might run into Detective Kingman there. He didn't want anything to stop him from talking to Brad Wyatt.

As it approached four o'clock he headed back to the Oak Ridge Cemetery and presented himself at the office at five minutes to four.

"I'm supposed to meet with Brad Wyatt," he told the clerk.

"Of course," the clerk said. "Mr. Glanville has arranged it. You can find him at the President's Tomb right..." He looked at his watch. "...now."

"Thanks."

Clint left the office and walked over to the tomb. There were people in the cemetery, visiting the graves of loved ones, setting down flowers, or actually there for burials. When he reached the tomb the doors were still open, and some people were milling about outside, either waiting to go in, or having just come out.

Clint remained outside to see what the people were going to do. Eventually, they wandered away from the tomb, and he went inside. He found a large man standing in front of the empty casket.

"Mr. Wyatt?"

The man turned.

"That's right." He had a heavy black beard that hung down to his deep chest. "Who are you?"

"My name's Clint Adams."

The big man was wearing a three-piece suit. He took a watch from his vest pocket.

"You're two minutes late."

"There were people outside," Clint said. "I waited to see if they were coming in."

"They were already inside," Wyatt said, putting his watch away. "I chased them out."

"We can talk, then."

Wyatt nodded.

"You wanted to know about the vandalism?"

"That's right."

"Well, that's easy." The man approached Clint, towered above him. He must have been six-and-a-half feet tall. He spread his arms. "Nothing was touched."

"The door..." Clint said.

"The lock was picked," Wyatt said, "and the President was taken, casket and all. Nothing else was damaged. If they were smart they would have wrecked the place."

"But there was no need," Clint said. "With the casket gone, you knew what they did."

"True," Wyatt said. "What I meant was, if Glanville was smart he would have wrecked the place, so we could claim vandalism. When the police came and we lied, it would have helped with the cover story."

"Too late for that now," Clint said.

"Yeah, it is. What can I tell you?"

"What have you found out?"

"There were no wagon tracks near the tomb," Wyatt said. "That means they carried the casket from the tomb, probably to a wagon further along where it wouldn't leave tracks."

"And how'd they get it out of Springfield? On a train?" Clint asked.

"Not a chance," Wyatt said. "I got to the station fast. Told the police I had a tip that the vandals were there. They couldn't have gotten the casket onto the train."

"Then they took it out by wagon," Clint said.

"There's lots of places in southern Illinois," Wyatt said, "caves, where they could have hidden it."

"Yeah," Clint said, "there are."

"What are you planning to do?" Wyatt asked. "Where are you going to look?"

Clint studied Wyatt. If there was an inside man, this was him.

"Not in Illinois," he said, "that's for sure."

"What are you talking about?"

"You don't need to know that," Clint said. "I'm at the Walnut Inn Hotel. I'll be there for two more days. If you think of anything that can help me, let me know."

"Look," Wyatt said, "take me with you. The President's safety was my job. Getting him back should be my job."

"Why weren't there armed guards on this tomb?" Clint asked.

"Why not ask the Army that?" Wyatt said. "Why should I have worried about his body being stolen if they weren't?"

"You're right," Clint said. "It's their fault, but it's also your fault. I've been charged with paying the ransom, and that's what I'm going to do."

"You're not gonna try to bring him back?"

"After I pay the ransom, if they turn the body over to me, I'll bring it back."

"And if they don't?"

"Then I think that'll be up to the Army, too, don't you?"

TWELVE

lint left the cemetery, but still didn't go back to the hotel. He found a place across the street, from where he could watch.

If Wyatt was the inside man, then he just told the body snatchers that his only job was to pay the ransom. They'd think they didn't have to worry about him bringing the body back, unless it was returned to him.

They'd also think he had the money with him. It made sense to expect them to try and take it from him. But before they could do that, Wyatt would have to deliver a message.

He planned to follow the security man. He'd either find out that Wyatt was part of the gang or he'd find out that the man was innocent.

At five o'clock the main gate to the cemetery closed.

At five-fifteen a smaller door in the wall next to the gate opened, and Brad Wyatt stepped out. He looked around, hitched up his gunbelt, and then started walking. Clint let him have a head start, and then fell into step behind him.

***

He doubted that the security man was going home. Once the cemetery was closed his job probably became even more important. So whatever he was on his way to do, he probably had to do it fast and get back before anyone noticed he was gone.

Of course, Clint was using his logic in assuming that the inside man would be Wyatt. It could also have been Glanville, the manager, or even the clerk. But he'd know soon enough if he had made the right call or not.

***

Wherever Wyatt was going, it was obviously walking distance. He made no move to wave down a carriage, or stop anywhere for a horse. His big, long stride took him along efficiently, getting him where he was going in a hurry.

Clint maintained a good distance behind Wyatt, but it really didn't matter. The security man was so intent on where he was going he never looked back. He had something on his mind, and he was in a hurry to get it off.

When he finally reached his destination it was a store smack in the center of a row of them. As the man went through the front door Clint got closer, saw that it was a carpenter's shop.

He looked through the front window, saw Wyatt approach a man standing behind a counter in a store filled with wooden furniture.

***

Sam Wentworth, master carpenter and former colonel in the Confederate Army, looked up and frowned as he saw Brad Wyatt enter the store.

"What the hell are you doin' here?" he demanded. "You ain't supposed to come heah."

"Take it easy," Wyatt said. "For all anybody knows I'm looking to have some furniture built."

"You're takin' a big chance."

"It needs to be taken," Wyatt said. "Clint Adams came to the cemetery today."

"Adams? The Gunsmith? So?"

"He was sent by Washington," Wyatt said. "He's the one who's gonna pay the ransom."

"We were told that already," Wentworth said.

"Yeah, but what's he doin' here?" Wyatt asked. "Why ain't he out in Colorado?"

"How do I know?" Wentworth said. "Maybe he just wanted to see the tomb before he heads out there."

"Well," Wyatt said, and then lowered his voice, "he's got to have the money with him."

"So?"

"He's stayin' at the Walnut Inn," Wyatt said. "Why don't we just take the money from him?"

"Take the money from the Gunsmith?" Wentworth asked. "Are you crazy?"

"He's only one man," Wyatt said. "I could take a few boys with me and—"

"What the hell are you doin', Wyatt?"

"Whataya mean?"

"Adams is gonna pay the money in Colorado, right?"

"Right."

"Did he say anything to make you think he wasn't?"

"No," Wyatt said. "He said that's his job."

"Not gettin' the casket back?"

"He said if the thieves offer him the casket after he pays the ransom he'd bring it back, but no, he didn't say that was part of his job. He just said he had to pay the ransom."

Wentworth, a tall, middle-aged man with well-muscled arms despite the fact that he was a slender man, spread his arms.

"Then what's the problem?" he asked. "Why take it from him when he's gonna give it to us?"

"I just thought—"

"You are not supposed to think, suh," Wentworth said. "You are supposed to do what you were paid to do, look the other way, which you did. There's no reason for you to panic like this."

Wyatt looked as if he had been slapped.

"I ain't panicked," he said, thrusting his jaw out, "I just thought we had a chance—"

"—to get killed trying to take the money from a man who's planning to give it to us anyway."

"Well..."

"Wyatt," Wentworth said, "go back to work. If Adams comes back to you, just answer his questions. Don't try to do any thinkin'. You ain't cut out for it, boy."

"Now look—" Wyatt started.

Wentworth reached out and patted Wyatt on the shoulder.

"Time for you to go, Wyatt."

The security man glared at the ex-military man for a moment, then turned and stormed angrily out of the store.

***

Clint saw Wyatt come out of the carpenter's shop. Even watching from across the street he could see how angry the man was. Whatever had transpired between him and the carpenter, he wasn't happy about it.

He decided not to follow Wyatt again. The man was most likely rushing back to work at the cemetery.

Clint's interest now was in the man in the carpenter's shop. Wyatt had probably gone there to tell the man that the Gunsmith was in town asking questions. If he went into the shop now, it would be pretty obvious that he had followed Wyatt there.

Clint saw that just down the street from him was a small café, which would afford him a good view of the front door of the carpenter's shop. He decided to have a cup of coffee and consider his next move, while watching the door.

THIRTEEN

He had two cups of coffee before the man from the shop came out and locked the door, obviously done for the day. When he walked away he did so at a leisurely pace.

Clint quickly paid for his coffee and left the café. The man from the shop was tall—though not as tall as Wyatt—and thin. He walked slowly, but took long strides. He also walked erect, with a military bearing.

If Clint was hoping the man would lead him to members of a gang that had stolen Lincoln's body, he was mistaken. Instead, the man simply went home to a house in a residential section of Springfield. It was a large two-story home with white columns. Without ever having heard the man's voice he was sure he would have a southern accent, probably an ex-Confederate officer—which would explain stealing Lincoln's body and holding it for ransom. There were still southerners who thought the Confederacy was coming back.

Clint only had one more day before he had to head for Colorado—and he intended on stopping in Denver before he continued on to Segundo. After all, Springfield was his idea. His job was to pay the ransom and bring back the body. But the question on his mind was why would the body snatcher take the body all the way to Colorado when they could hide it right here in Springfield?

He decided it was finally time for him to go back to his hotel.

***

"There you are!" Angie said, from behind the desk. "I was starting to think you got lost."

"I took a good look at your city," Clint said.

"All day?"

"I walked slowly," he said. "Can you go to Frieda's for supper?"

"Yes," she said, "in about half an hour."

"Then I'm going to go to my room and get washed up," he said. "That is, unless I can get a bath?"

"We have room in the back," she said, "with bath-tubs. Do you want hot water?"

"Definitely."

"Then I'll have a hot bath prepared for you. Come back down in about ten minutes."

"That's great."

Clint went up to his room to get a fresh shirt and socks, sat on the bed for a few moments to consider what—if anything—he had found out that day that was helpful.

The fact that he had followed Brad Wyatt to a carpenter's store, and then the carpenter to his house, did not positively confirm that the theft of Lincoln's body had been an inside job and that these two men had been involved. But it seemed likely to Clint. He didn't think the theft could have occurred without an inside man, and the head of security was a natural for that position.

If he didn't find out anything for sure the next day, he was going to have to leave Springfield and head

West to Colorado. But maybe he could get Washington to send someone else to follow up his finding—or his suspicions. After all, the government could not possibly be intending to pay the ransom without trying to bring the thieves to justice.

He stood up to go down for his bath when there was a knock on his door.

"I was just on the way down—" he was saying as he opened the door, expecting to see Angie. Instead he found himself looking at Detective Dan Kingman.

"Mr. Adams," he said, "am I disturbing you?"

"Well, I was just on my way down for a bath," Clint said.

"Well, I won't keep you long," Kingman said. "May I come in?"

"Sure."

Clint backed up and allowed the man to enter.

"I checked the register downstairs, and you did, indeed, check in as Clint Adams."

"But that doesn't prove that I am Clint Adams."

"Not at all. You said you had some letters?"

Clint walked to his saddlebags, rummaged inside, and came out with a couple of letters addressed to him. He handed them to the detective.

Kingman looked at the envelopes, asked, "Can I open them?"

"Sure, they're not very interesting, though."

Kingman took the letters out and scanned them, not really reading them, then folded them and put them back into the envelopes before handing them back.

"I suppose there'd be no reason for you to have those if you weren't who you say you are."

"I don't think so."

"I also checked the livery stable across the street to

see your horse," Kingman explained. "That animal is almost as famous as you are."

"Is he? I don't think I knew that."

"So you have the Gunsmith's mail and the Gunsmith's horse, so I suppose it's a pretty safe bet you're the Gunsmith."

"Thank you," Clint said. "Did I mention my bath was supposed to be a hot one?"

"Why don't we walk down together?" Kingman suggested.

"Fine with me."

They left the room and started down the hall.

"Did you have that meeting with the head of security at the cemetery, Wyatt?"

"I did."

"What did you think of him?"

"Well, to tell the truth," Clint said, "I don't know how vandals could have pulled this off without him."

Kingman looked surprised.

"You think it was an inside job?"

"I do," Clint said. "Why does that surprise you?"

"It doesn't," Kingman said. "I just thought I was the only one who thought so."

"If you think it was an inside job, does that mean you're investigating further?"

"Let's say I'm still looking into it when I have a chance," Kingman said. "My chief is not convinced I'm right."

They went down the steps and reached the lobby. Angie was still behind the desk with a thin young man who was probably relieving her.

"Well, Detective, I suggest you look a little deeper into who Brad Wyatt's friends are."

"You have someone in mind?"

"I don't have a name," Clint said, "but I might before I leave town."

"Then by all means," Kingman said, "stop by the station and let me know before you leave."

"I'll do that."

They shook hands and the detective walked out the front door.

"Are you ready for your bath?" Angie asked.

"I'm ready," Clint said. "Lead the way."

FOURTEEN

Angie showed Clint into a room with a steaming bath-tub in the center of the floor. There was a chair in the corner, and she dropped his towels and cloths onto it.

"If you don't mind," he said, and moved the chair closer to the tub, "I'll need to hang my gunbelt on that, within easy reach."

"I'm sorry," she said. "I didn't realize... do you have it close to you at all times?"

"Yes," he said, "at all times."

"Even asleep?"

"Hanging on the bedpost," he said.

"That must be a difficult way to live."

He shrugged. "I'm used to it now. It's become part of me."

"I suppose so," she said. "Here's your soap." She handed him a brand new bar.

"Thank you."

"Take your time," she said. "This tub is designed to hold the heat in for a long time."

"That's good to know."

"Just let me know when you're finished," she said.

'I will," he said. "Thank you."

She didn't move.

"If you leave," he said, "I'll get undressed."

"Oh, yeah," she said, "sorry." She backed out of the

63

room and closed the door.

Clint got undressed, put his clothes on the chair, hung his gunbelt on the back, and eased himself into the hot water. He sighed as the heat began to seep into his muscles. Rather than wash immediately he just soaked for a while, letting the heat do its work.

***

Detective Dan Kingman got back to the police station and immediately went to the Chief's office.

"Chief?" he said, knocking on the open door.

The man looked up and waved him in.

"Sit," the Chief said. "What have you got?"

"I went to the Walnut Inn, checked on the bona fides of the man who said he was Clint Adams."

"And?"

"It appears he was telling the truth," Kingman said. "He has letters in that name."

"Is that all?"

"No," Kingman said. "I checked at the livery across from the hotel. If he's not Adams, he's riding Adams' horse."

"How do you know?"

"The Gunsmith rides a big Darley Arabian," Kingman said. "Everybody knows that. It's not a horse you see everywhere."

"All right," the Chief said, "so the Gunsmith is in town. What does that tell us?"

"He also agrees with my thinking," Kingman said. "About the vandalism."

"That it's an inside job?"

"Yes," the detective said. "He indicated that he might have a name for me tomorrow."

"And when is he leaving town?"

"Very soon," Kingman said. "He originally said he was only staying a couple of days. I assume he's leaving the day after tomorrow."

"Well," the Chief said, "let's hope he gets you that name before he leaves, then."

"Yes, sir."

The Chief sat back in his chair.

"You know there's a short list of who could be the inside man, don't you?"

"Yessir," Kingman said. "Glanville, the manager; David Rabe, the clerk; and Brad Wyatt, head of security."

"Wyatt wore a badge in Springfield for a while," the Chief said.

"Until you took it away from him."

"I came in and swept out all the corruption," the older man said. "He was knee-deep in it."

"Yes, sir."

"If there's an inside man," the Chief said, "he's my best bet."

"I agree."

"Have you spent any time on him?"

"Followed him for a day or two, but he only went to work and back home again, with a stop for some place to eat and have a drink."

"And who'd he talk to?"

"Nobody," Kingman said. "From what I can see, he's got no friends."

"Everybody has somebody they talk to, Dan," the Chief said. "Women?"

"Just whores."

"All right," the Chief said, "let's see if Mr. Adams actually comes through with a name for you."

Kingman nodded and rose to leave.

"Remind me again why you think something other than vandalism happened?" the Chief said.

"Because," Kingman said, "it's kind of hard to have vandalism without any damage, Chief."

"Ah, yes," the Chief said, nodding, "you did make that point before."

FIFTEEN

Clint was still soaking in the tub, his eyes closed but his ears very alert. He heard the door open quietly, and as someone crept toward the tub he quickly reached for his gun, drew it, and pointed it...

...at Angie.

"Oh!" she said, startled. "My God!"

"Sorry," he said, turning the gun away from her. "You shouldn't sneak up on me like that."

"I—I was trying to surprise yon."

"Well, you did," he said, holstering the gun.

She stood there, apparently now undecided about whatever it was she was going to do.

"I'm not done with my bath yet," he said.

"I—I was hoping you weren't."

"Why?"

"Well... I know you'll be leaving tomorrow," she said, "and, you know, we talked about me doing some of the things I wanted to do, like travelling, and I, well..."

"What is it, Angie?"

She came closer to the tub, looked into it. He saw where her eyes were going, and realized his cock was erect and poking up out of the water. The spongy head gleamed wetly at her.

"I—I've decided to be more bold," she said.

"Angie."

67

She got down on her knees next to the tub, reached in, and took hold of him. Slowly, she began to stroke him.

"I'm not a virgin," she said, "in case you were wondering, but... I'm not all that experienced, either."

"You seem to be doing pretty well," he said. "Uh, what about your father? What if—"

"He's not working today," she said. "Besides, Benny's behind the desk and he said he'd keep watch."

"Does Benny know why he's keeping watch?"

"Well, yes... he's my boyfriend. He'd do anything for me?"

"And... he doesn't mind?"

"I explained it to him," she said. "He understands."

She reached into the water with her other hand to cup his balls.

"Sounds like you better keep him," he said, tightly. "Sounds like a really good boyfriend."

"He is," she said. "He's sweet."

Abruptly she stood up, shrugged, and her cotton dress fell to the floor. She was prepared for this, naked underneath. Her body was young, smooth, and firm. The nipples of her pert breasts were brown and rigid, the bush between her legs plentiful and dark. She stepped into the tub, which was large enough to accommodate both of them.

She sat across from him, stretched her legs out on the inside of his so that he could feel her smooth skin. She leaned forward and took his penis into both hands again. As she stroked him he reached out and touched her breasts and nipples, causing her to catch her breath.

The water was still hot, but the temperature was something neither of them seemed concerned with at the moment. She was so intent on his penis that she got to her

68

knees in the water to get closer to it, began to stroke the length of him with both hands. He caressed her breasts, pinched her nipples, then reached into the water to poke into her wet bush and stroke her. She gasped, her body jerking as if she had been struck by lightning.

"Here," he said, reaching for her, "come here..."

He pulled her into his lap, pinning his cock beneath her. She wriggled her butt, liking the way he felt beneath her, but then he slid his hands beneath her butt, lifted her, and slid right into her with ease.

"Ooh," she said, and started sliding up and down on him, splashing water from the tub to the floor.

He sat back in the tub with his hands resting lightly on her hips, letting her do the work. The bouncing up-and-down became more and more energetic, causing more and more splashing, and her breath began to come in great gulps. When her eyes rolled up in her head he thought she might pass out, but instead she began to tremble and bounce uncontrollably on him, so he took hold of her more firmly to hold her in place until the waves of passion passed and she slumped against him. Moving her head she kissed him, and the kiss went on for a long time until she broke it, gasping for breath.

"Oh God," she said, "what was that?"

"What was... you mean, you never had that happen to you before? With Benny?"

"No," she gasped, "I've never felt anything like that before in my life."

"Oh, sweet girl," he said, "we have a lot to talk about."

"Talk," she said, drawing back and looking at him very seriously. Her lips were still swollen, her nostrils still flaring. "I don't wanna talk, Mr. Gunsmith." She moved her hips. He was still inside her, and felt himself begin to stir again. "I want to do it again!"

SIXTEEN

They did go again, and afterward Clint disengaged from the young woman, who clung to him, asking for more.

"Later," he told her, "in a bed, where we can do it properly."

"That wasn't properly?" she asked. "It gets better than that?"

"A lot better."

"Oh my God!"

He got dressed and strapped on his gun. She dried herself, then pulled her dress back on.

"I have to stay behind to clean up," she said.

"You should," he said. "You made this mess."

She giggled and said, "Yes, I did, didn't I?"

He kissed her and said, "I'll see you later, Angie."

"Hey, you were gonna tell me stories over supper!" she complained.

"Well, I don't have time for supper right now," he said. "You sort of took up my free time, already."

"I'll come to your room later, then," she promised.

He didn't bother trying to dissuade her. The time in the tub had been very pleasant, and he was looking forward to taking her to a real bed. She was very energetic, and eager to learn.

Maybe she was younger than he thought after all.

***

Clint went out through the lobby and, judging from the glare he drew from Benny the clerk, thought that maybe the young man wasn't such an understanding boyfriend after all.

He didn't want to have supper with Angie because he still needed time to think over his next move. He walked to Frieda's and got a table, ordered a steak from Arthur, who asked after Angie.

"Whatever you do, don't tell her I was here," Clint said. "I just needed to have a meal with some quiet."

"Yes," Arthur said, "she's quite a talker. I understand."

Arthur brought him a pot of coffee while he waited.

Clint was thinking about the man from the carpenter's shop. He wanted to give the name to Detective Kingman, but he didn't know it. He thought about going to the man's neighborhood to try and find out the name, but then took it one step further. Why not knock on the man's door, maybe shake him up a bit if he was, in fact, involved in stealing Lincoln's body.

The steak came and for the time it took him to consume the meal he was very happy to concentrate on nothing else, it was that good. When the steak was gone he spent time over pie and coffee convincing himself he was making the right move.

When he was done he paid his check, said goodbye to Arthur, and headed for the carpenter's house.

***

First he visited some neighbors under the pretext of looking for a nonexistent person.

"I thought he lived in that house over there, but I'm

not sure," he said to one lady.

"Oh, that's Colonel Wentworth's house."

"Colonel?"

The old woman grimaced and said, "He was a colonel in the Confederate Army. Now he's a carpenter, but he still demands to be called Colonel. Lotta nerve, you ask me."

"I guess."

"Colonel Samuel Wentworth," she said with distaste. "Can ya imagine?" Then she frowned at him. "You ain't a southerner, are ya?"

"No, Ma'am," he said. "Not me."

"Yeah, well..." she said, dubiously, and closed the door in his face.

But he had enough.

***

He knocked on the door of the Colonel's house. He was surprised when it was answered by a handsome, expensively dressed woman in her mid-forties. In her youth she must have been quite a beauty. Now her beauty had ripened into something merely lovely.

"Yes?"

"I hope I'm not disturbing your dinner?" he asked.

"No," she said, "we've finished. We were just having an after dinner drink."

"Good," he said. "I'd like to see your husband, the Colonel."

"Only he calls himself the Colonel."

"You don't?"

"No."

"Why not?"

She leaned in and lowered her voice as if imparting

a secret.

"He's not a colonel anymore."

He lowered his voice to match hers. "Can I see him?"

"Why not?" she said. "It might be interesting. Follow me, please."

They closed the door and he followed her into the house. She took him to a large, well-furnished living room that Clint doubted had been furnished with money earned from a carpenter's shop.

In the center of the room sat a tall man seated in a plush chair, dressed in a Confederate officer's uniform—a colonel's uniform. He had a drink in one hand.

"Samuel," the woman said, "a man to see you."

"Thank you, darling," the man said. "Would you get Mr. Adams a glass of brandy, please?"

"Adams?" she asked.

"Clint Adams," the man said, "otherwise known as the Gunsmith."

"And you are?" Clint asked.

"Wentworth," the man said, "Colonel Samuel Wentworth."

"Only you can't be a colonel in the Confederate Army anymore," Clint said, accepting the drink from the woman, "because there isn't a Confederate Army anymore."

"I beg to differ," Wentworth said. "I never recognized General Lee's surrender, or the dissolution of the Confederacy."

"That doesn't mean you can still use Confederate script, does it?" Clint asked.

"He's got you there, darling," his wife said.

"This is my wife," Wentworth said, "Gemma."

"Lovely name," Clint said.

"Thank you."

74

"Gemma, darling," Wentworth said, "would you leave Mr. Adams and me alone?"

"Not a chance," she said, "I want to see this... dear."

Wentworth glared at his wife, then looked at Clint and said, "What can I do for the Gunsmith?"

SEVENTEEN

"How did you know who I was?" Clint asked.

"The Gunsmith comes to Springfield?" Wentworth said. "Did you think that would be a secret?"

"Yes, but how did you know—"

"You're wearing a gun," Wentworth said. "They're trying to keep men from wearing guns in the city. But you... that would mean your instant death, wouldn't it?"

Clint had seen other men in town wearing guns. Granted, not as many as he might see in Abilene or Virginia City, but enough to negate Wentworth's logic.

"You knew who I was because Brad Wyatt told you."

Wentworth smiled. "You followed him."

"I did."

The Colonel shook his head. "Stupid."

"Are you calling the Gunsmith stupid, dear?" Gemma asked.

"I think he means Wyatt," Clint said.

"Oh," Gemma said.

"Does Gemma know what this is about?" Clint asked.

"Yes, she does."

"It's stupid," she said.

"Gemma!"

"He asked."

"You're supposed to be on your way to Segundo to

pay a ransom," he said to Clint.

"Why don't I just pay you and save myself the trip?" Clint suggested.

"That's not how it is set up."

"Why not?" Clint asked. "It would be so much simpler, wouldn't it?"

"If only we could do things the simple way," Wentworth said.

Clint was sure that was some kind of observation on the war.

"Ah," Clint said, "you don't have the body."

Wentworth didn't react.

"It's not here in Springfield?"

Nothing.

"Why take it all the way to Colorado?" Clint asked. "It doesn't make sense."

"Neither did the war," Wentworth said. "Or the foolish way it ended. Our way of life in the South was working so well for us, and then Lincoln—"

"Please, Samuel," Gemma said, cutting him off. Clint had a feeling she had done so many, many times before. "Not this again."

Wentworth fell silent and glared at his wife, then looked at Clint.

"Gemma," Wentworth said, "would you see Mr. Adams to the door?"

"It would be my great pleasure, dear," she said. "Mr. Adams?"

Clint put his glass down untouched and stood up. "Thank you." He was talking to her, not him.

He followed her to the front door. She opened it and stood aside, her drink still in her hand.

"Goodnight, Gemma."

"Wait," she said, as he started out.

He stopped. She stepped to him and kissed him on the mouth. She tasted of brandy, and something else that only she could taste of. She broke the kiss and licked his lower lip before stepping back.

"What was that for?" he asked.

"Because I don't have time to fuck you," she said.

He took a step, put his arm around her, pulled her to him and kissed her deeply. When the kiss was done they were both out of breath.

"Oh my," she said.

"My loss," he said, and left.

EIGHTEEN

lint went back to his hotel. When he arrived there was activity in the lobby. Angie and her father were there, with Benny the clerk, and two policemen. And coming down the stairs from the second floor was Detective Kingman, who spotted Clint coming in the door.

"Mr. Adams," he said, "come on in. You'll find this very interesting."

"What's going on?" Clint asked.

He and Kingman met in the center of the lobby, with the others standing on the outskirts.

"Apparently," Kingman said, "somebody broke into your room."

"Is that a fact? Did they get anything?"

"Well," Kingman said, "we'll need you to tell us that. Would you come up?"

"Lead the way, Detective."

As they walked past Angie's father he said to Clint, "I'm so sorry, Mr. Adams..."

"It's not your fault, sir," Clint said. "Don't worry about it."

He followed Kingman upstairs and down the hall to his room, where the door was wide open. Inside the room had been torn apart. Even the mattress was on the floor, having been sliced open.

"What a mess," Clint said.

"Can you tell if anything's missing?"

"Well," Clint said, "I didn't have that much to begin with."

He went through his saddlebags and put them down.

"My saddlebags are still here, so's my rifle," Clint said. "That's about all I had."

"Yes," Kingman said, "but what did someone think you had?"

"Damned if I know," Clint said. "Did they break into any other rooms?"

"No," Kingman said, "just yours. That's why I'm wondering what they thought they'd find."

"I can't help you," Clint said. "Maybe they just knew where my room was and wanted a memento."

"Just wanted to say they stole something from the Gunsmith, huh?"

Clint shrugged.

"Except you say they didn't get anything."

"Did someone scare them off?"

"No," Kingman said. "The owner's daughter said she came up and found the door open and the room a shambles."

"I see," Clint said, still looking around. "Well, I don't see anything missing, Detective. Maybe they were just vandals."

"You mean like Lincoln's Tomb?"

Clint looked at the man.

"Yes," he said, "exactly like Lincoln's Tomb."

"Uh-huh. Why don't we go back downstairs?"

The two men walked down the hall, and down the steps to the lobby in silence.

"All right, sir," Kingman said to Angie's father, "we've done all we can."

"Thank you, Deputy."

"Detective."

"Yes, of course," the man said. "Detective."

Kingman looked at Clint.

"I'm sure this gentleman will see that you get a new room."

"Of course," the manager said, "of course. Benny? Another key for Mr. Adams."

Benny didn't look happy, but he turned and grabbed another key and handed it to his boss, who in turn handed it to Clint.

"Goodnight, gentlemen," Kingman said, then executed a slight bow and said to Angie, "Miss."

He left, with the other officers following him.

Angie's father said, "I'm terribly sorry—"

"That's all right," Clint said, "not your fault. I'll just move my things to the other room." He nodded to Angie and headed for the stairs.

On the way he heard the man say to Angie, "We've got to get up there and clean that room!"

"Yes, Papa."

***

Clint moved his belongings to the new room, which did not have a window overlooking the street. He sat on the bed and thought about it. The only person he could think of who might have ransacked his room was Brad Wyatt, looking for the ransom money. In fact, he might have even been doing it while Clint was talking with Colonel Wentworth.

Wyatt must have been disappointed to find nothing of value in the room. The question was did Wentworth send him, or did the security man act on his own?

Clint had one more day in Springfield. Or he could

simply board a train the next morning and leave. It was obvious he was going to have to make the trek to Colorado to pay the ransom. He decided to wait until morning to make the decision.

He decided to do some reading and found himself hoping that Angie did not come to his room as she had promised. Maybe her father would keep her occupied.

But he was unable to distract himself with Mark Twain, found himself just sitting, pondering his next move. How smart had it been to reveal himself to Colonel Wentworth? And yet Wentworth and his colleagues all knew who was bringing the ransom money. Facing the man here in Springfield had probably done no harm. But maybe it was now time to get to the task at hand.

Yes, he determined that he should leave in the morning.

As he was preparing himself for bed there was a knock on the door. Thinking it was Angie, he nevertheless carried his gun to the door.

"Angie, I'm afraid—" He stopped short when he saw Gemma Wentworth, wrapped in a capelike coat.

"Sorry," she said, "not Angie. May I come in?"

Clint peeked each way in the hall to determine that she was alone.

"I'm quite alone, I assure you."

"Come in."

She entered, moving past him with a swish of skirts, trailing a heady scent behind her. As with the taste of her when he kissed her—or she him—this was a smell singular to her.

She turned to face him.

"I'm sorry, but I couldn't just let you go."

"Let me go?"

"Let you leave Springfield," she said. "Are you going tomorrow?"

"I was actually going to stay another day, but I've just decided tonight to leave in the morning."

"Then it's good that I came when I did."

"Do you have something for me?" he asked. "Some... information?"

"Information, perhaps," she said, "but something? Definitely. And something for me."

She reached to the tie that held her cape in place, pulled it. The cape fell away, revealing the top of her frock to be plunging. Her shoulders were bare, as were the slopes of her generous breasts.

"I was beautiful in my youth," she said.

"You're beautiful now," he said.

"I'm happy you think so." She reached behind her with both hands, causing her breasts to jut forward. She undid the dress with both hands and it dropped to the floor, leaving only a silky undergarment. With a whisper of silk she discarded that as well and stood naked before him.

Gloriously naked, a body that was full and firm, breasts like ripe fruits...

"After kissing you," she said, "I needed more... much more."

NINETEEN

Clint took her hand with his free hand, guided her toward the bed. As he slid his gun back into the holster on the bedpost, he could feel the heat coming off her body.

With both hands now free he reached for her breasts, cupped them in his hands, enjoying the weight of them. Her nipples were light brown, the skin around them dappled with goose flesh. She closed her eyes and gave herself up to his touch.

"What about your husband?" he asked.

"He has other things on his mind," she said. "Besides, he and I are married in name only. There is nothing between us."

"Well, that's good..."

He lifted her breasts to his lips, kissed the flesh, licked the nipples, then bit them lightly, lovingly.

"Oooh," she said, "it has been a long time."

He could tell. She was already wet, and he could smell her readiness. He continued to caress her breasts with one hand, and slid the other between her legs. As expected, she was soaking and sensitive. She gasped as he slid his finger along her moist slit.

Abruptly, he pulled her to him, kissed her soundly, then turned and lowered her onto the bed. As she lay there on her back she watched him undress, and when his rigid penis came into view her eyes widened.

"It *has* been a long time," she said. "But... I've never seen anything... you're beautiful."

He crawled over her, lowered himself onto her, and guided the head of his cock to her wet portal. He pierced her with ease, and she immediately wrapped her legs around his waist, locking him into place.

They began to move together, her moans coming loud and long in his ear. Just for a moment he wondered if others in the building could hear her, but then decided it didn't matter. The only thing that mattered was what was happening between them.

"Oh God, yes," she groaned. "That's it... ooh-ooh-ooooh... don't stop..."

"Why would I stop?" he breathed into her ear.

She reached around to hold him by the cheeks of his ass, pulling on him each time he thrusted into her. He, in turn, slid his hands beneath her, cupping the cheeks of her butt and doing the same.

Before long they were both grunting with the effort of fucking, the bed rail banging against the wall, the bed fairly leaping off the floor, and then she bit his shoulder to keep from screaming, and he stifled his own rising shout, and it was as if that effort only intensified the sensations they were each feeling, eventually leaving them both totally drained...

***

"My God," she said, a little later. "I'm so glad I decided to come here."

"So am I."

She reached for him as they lay side by side, took his penis in her hand, just holding it. It grew semi-hard just from her touch.

"I wish you weren't leaving tomorrow."

"I have to leave," he said, "and you know why."

"I know remarkably little," she said, "beyond the fact that you're paying a ransom, and what that ransom is for."

"So you can't tell me who else is involved?"

"Aside from my husband and that idiot, Wyatt? No. My husband is involved with a band of zealots who can't admit the Confederacy is gone." She stroked his cock, making it harden even more. "You should be very careful. I believe they'll all mad as hatters."

"I'm always careful."

"I have to get back to the house," she said, "but first..."

She rolled over, lowered herself to his crotch. She continued to stroke his cock until it was nice and hard, and then lowered her mouth over him. She engulfed him, hotly, wetly, and began to suck, moaning as she did so, and kept it up until he grunted and exploded into her mouth...

***

He watched her dress, also wishing he wasn't leaving in the morning and that she could stay until then. Angie had been a nice diversion in the tub, but Gemma was a real woman, whose hungers had been reawakened after years of unhappiness with her husband.

"I do have something else to tell you," she said, patting her hair into place.

"And what's that?"

"My husband is an old goat, and so are some of the others," she said, "but they have managed to convince younger men to join them. In essence, they've recruited new soldiers into the Confederacy, so you have to be very careful. I suggest that before you go anywhere near Segundo, you recruit some help yourself."

"Thank you," he said. "I was already considering that."

"Good."

She went to the bed, kissed him quickly, and backed away as he reached for her.

"I have to leave now, or not leave 'til morning."

"That'd be okay with me."

"I don't want to give my husband a reason to come after you before you leave."

"Would he be jealous?"

"It wouldn't be jealousy," she said. "Just that you had something that belonged to him."

"Why don't you leave?"

"And go where?" she asked. "Do what? No, I'm trapped where I am. But I thank you for giving me moments of freedom, Clint. Just do me a favor."

"What's that?"

"Don't get yourself killed."

"I'll do my best, Gemma."

She blew him another kiss and slipped out the door.

TWENTY

He woke the next morning feeling oddly refreshed after an energetic night. When he went downstairs to check out, Angie's father was behind the desk.

"Leaving early, sir?" he asked.

"Yes."

"I'm sorry about what happened—"

"That has nothing to do with it," Clint said. "I simply have to go."

"Of course."

"Is Angie around? I'd like to say goodbye."

"I'm afraid not, sir," he said. "She went up to see if your new room was satisfactory, and when she came down she was quite upset."

Uh-oh. That probably meant she knew about Gemma.

"Well," Clint said, "please say goodbye for me."

"Of course."

Clint paid his bill, went across the street to get Eclipse, who seemed to be in fine shape.

"He eats more than any two horses," the hostler said.

"Do you want to charge me extra?" Clint asked.

"Hell, no," the man said. "My pleasure to have him in my place."

"Thank you," Clint said.

He left the livery, started walking Eclipse toward the train station. He didn't know what time the first train left and would need to make arrangements to get Eclipse onto a stock car.

When he got to the station and went inside he found Detective Dan Kingman sitting on a bench. The man rose as he entered.

"Waiting for me?"

"I am."

"What made you think I was leaving today?"

"Let's just call it a hunch."

"Well, I have to find out when the first train leaves and make arrangements for my horse. What can I do for you?"

"You said something about having a name for me before you left town."

"I did say that, didn't I?"

"Don't tell me you're gonna disappoint me?"

"No," Clint said, "I don't think what I have to tell you will be a disappointment."

"That's good."

"I'm fairly certain Brad Wyatt was the inside man at the cemetery."

"I suspected as much," Wentworth said. "That's nothing new."

"Well, you might look into a man who has a carpenter's shop here in town. His name is Samuel Wentworth. Actually, he calls himself Colonel Wentworth."

"Colonel?"

"A Confederate colonel."

"Really?"

"There are still those who haven't accepted the outcome of the war."

"I hate zealots."

"I know what you mean."

"Anything else?"

"I believe Wentworth's wife is an innocent," Clint added, for Gemma's sake.

"I'll keep that in mind." Kingman put his hand out, and Clint shook it. "Thanks."

"My pleasure."

"I'm sure I shouldn't ask if you enjoyed your stay here in Springfield."

"Actually," Clint said, thinking of Angie and Gemma, "it had its moments."

The detective left the station as Clint stepped to the window to make his travel arrangements.

Next stop: Denver.

TWENTY-ONE

Denver, CO

Talbot Roper sat back in his chair and considered everything his friend had just told him.

"Why the heck would they bring the body and the casket all the way out here?" he asked.

"I have the same question," Clint said.

"There's no way they could have removed the body from the casket," Roper went on, "not after all this time."

"Agreed. If they traveled with it, they had to travel with the entire thing."

"You know what I think?" Roper said.

"No," Clint said, "but that's what I want to know, Tal, what you think."

"I don't think they intend to give the body back when you pay the ransom," the detective said. "I think if you want that body back you're going to have to take it."

"Makes sense to me."

Roper waved to the waiter for the check but when it came Clint grabbed it.

The two friends left the restaurant and the hotel to walk aimlessly.

"Okay, my friend," Roper said, "what do you want from me besides my opinion?"

"First, I'm wondering if the thieves came all the way

by wagon," Clint said, "or if at some point they put the casket on a train."

"I can check on that."

"Then I need to know what the situation is in Segundo," Clint added. "Is there any law-and-order there? Or is it an outlaw hold?"

"I can find that out, too," Roper assured him. "Anything else?"

"Well," Clint said, "like you said, I think I'm going to have to take the body back. I was kind of hoping you'd ride down there with me and watch my back."

"You know I will," Roper said. "What about Masterson? Can we get hold of him?"

"I sent some telegrams, but got no word back," Clint said, shaking his head. "I don't know where Bat is, or what he's up to."

"And Earp?"

"I think he's in Alaska."

"So it's just you and me?"

"I was hoping that it was at least you and me, Tal," Clint said.

"Well, lucky for you I cleared my desk," Roper said. "I have no active cases keeping me in Denver. When do you want to leave?"

"Tomorrow," Clint said, "if you can get all the information we need by then."

"Well, I'll need to work all day today to get it," Roper said, "so we better say goodbye now and I'll see you in the morning."

The two friends shook hands and separated there on the street.

"I'll meet you in front of your hotel with my horse and supplies."

"I want to travel light."

"Don't worry, I know how you work, Clint," Roper assured him. "I'll just have supplies divided into two sacks, one for you, one for me."

"Okay, Tal."

Roper crossed the street and hurried off to work on the information Clint wanted.

Clint went back to his hotel.

***

Feeling as if he was wasting the rest of the day Clint went back out a couple of hours later and walked to the nearest telegraph office. He sent several telegrams, still trying to locate his friend, Bat Masterson, and then sent one to Detective Kingman in Springfield, inquiring about Wentworth and Wyatt. He asked the clerk to send the replies to his hotel as soon as each came in, and not to wait for them all.

"Yessir," the man said. "I'll take care of it."

Clint left, walked back to the hotel.

***

He was in the dining room having lunch when the first reply arrived. A boy appeared at the doorway to the dining room, spoke to one of the waiters, then was allowed to approach Clint's table.

"Got a telegram for you, Mister," the boy said, "that is, if you're the Gunsmith."

"I am."

"Golly," the boy said, staring.

"Are you going to give it to me?" Clint asked.

The boy continued to stare, but held the telegram out to him.

"Thanks," Clint said, handing the boy a coin. "Here

you go."

"Gee, thanks, Mister."

"Hang around the telegraph office a little longer," Clint said. "There might be more."

"Thanks!"

The boy turned and ran out.

Clint looked at the telegram. It was from the detective in Springfield.

BOTH MEN GONE. SUGGEST YOU WATCH YOUR BACK. KINGMAN.

He folded the telegram and put it in his pocket. So both Wentworth and Wyatt had left town. Were they headed for Segundo also? Had that been the plan all along, or had Clint's actions influenced theirs?

He certainly didn't have to be told to watch his back.

***

He wasn't finished with his lunch when the boy appeared a second time. This time he had two telegrams. Clint gave him two coins, but was disappointed at the contents. Both informed him that his messages had not reached Bat Masterson.

Where the hell was Bat these days, he wondered. It would certainly make him feel safer to go to Segundo to face a group of disgruntled old Graybacks with two of his friends watching his back instead of one.

***

Still feeling as if he was wasting time, Clint sat in the lobby of the hotel rather than in his room. At least he had people to watch as they checked in or out, or simply came in to eat in the dining room. He was seated there when the desk clerk came over.

"Sir, a message for you." The man handed him a slip of paper.

Clint had seen a boy come into the hotel, but it was not the same boy who had brought him his telegram, so he'd ignored him.

"Thank you."

He opened it. It was from Roper, asking him to meet him for dinner at a steak restaurant called Mason's. Roper supplied the address.

At least this gave him something to do, and Roper had probably come up with the information Clint needed. He stood to go to his room to get dressed for dinner, then realized he really had nothing but trail clothes with him. So instead of going to his room he left the hotel and asked the doorman where the nearest place was he could buy a suit.

TWENTY-TWO

He arrived at Mason's on time, stepped down from the cab he'd taken from the hotel and paid the driver.

Roper was waiting at a table, waved a white napkin so Clint could see him.

"I was glad to hear from you," Clint said, sitting. "I felt like I was just wasting time."

"I was able to get the information I needed quickly," Roper said.

"About the train? Or Segundo?"

"Both." A waiter came over. "Steak?" Roper asked Clint.

"What else?"

"Two steak dinners, Andre," Roper said, "and two mugs of beer."

"Yes, Mr. Roper," the waiter said, "right away." He smiled at Clint and walked away.

"What have you got for me?"

"About two weeks ago a casket did come in on the train," Roper said.

"Do we know what happened to it?"

"No," Roper said, "beyond the fact that it was offloaded onto a buckboard. Nobody knows where it was going."

"It didn't go to any of the funeral homes in the city?" Clint asked.

"No."

"So that was Lincoln, then."

"Seems so."

"How far is it from here to Segundo?"

"Pretty far. A couple of hundred miles."

"Could they have gotten it there in two weeks?"

"Maybe just."

"That's what I was thinking."

"And it could certainly be there by the time we get there," Roper said.

Clint nodded.

"What about Segundo?" Clint asked. "What are we looking at there?"

"They don't have their own lawman," Roper said. "I believe the sheriff from Trinidad would be called in if they needed one."

"Bat was sheriff of Trinidad for a while, some years back," Clint said. "Do we know who the sheriff is now?"

"No."

"Well," Clint said, "maybe we should stop in there first."

"Sounds like an idea."

The waiter came with their steak dinners and beers and they suspended conversation for a while—at least until they had made a dent in their dinners.

***

Both men had slowed down, but had no intention of leaving any of the meat behind.

"I tried a few more telegrams looking for Bat, but no luck," Clint said.

"I could draft a couple of men from here in Denver," Roper said.

Clint made a face.

"I'd really rather not make that ride with men I don't know," Clint said, "even though I know you'd recommend good men."

"I get it," Roper said. "I think the two of us can handle this."

"There's no telling how many Graybacks are going to be involved."

"I think a couple of old Bluebellies can handle it," Roper said.

Clint picked up his beer, raised it and said, "I'll drink to that."

TWENTY-THREE

hen Clint came out the next morning Roper was waiting there with his horse. The Denver House had their own stable, so they walked around to it and Roper waited outside while Clint settled his bill and saddled Eclipse.

"You're finally going to get to stretch your legs, big boy," he said.

He walked Eclipse outside, where Roper was mounted on his steeldust and waiting.

"I always forget how impressive that horse is," he commented.

"I know," Clint said, mounting up. "He hasn't had much chance to run lately, though."

"He'll get plenty now," Roper said. "It's a little over two hundred miles."

"Let's go," Clint said.

***

They left Denver, riding south, each with a sack of supplies tied to their saddles. Clint liked to travel with only the bare essentials when he was tracking someone, or riding the trail for any reason—frying pan, coffee pot, coffee, bacon, beans, and dried beef jerky. Sometimes canned peaches.

They chatted during the ride, catching up on each other's lives. Roper had worked some interesting cases and enjoyed talking about them. Clint liked talking about his experiences less, tended to gloss over most of the facts. Therefore, he tended to let Roper talk on and on for as long as he wanted.

***

They pushed and camped for the night about eight miles north of Colorado Springs.

"We've got no reason to stop in town tomorrow," Clint said. "We can bypass Colorado Springs very easily."

"It's your call, Boss," Roper said, chewing on a piece of bacon.

"Don't call me that."

"Well," Roper said, "this is your job, so you make all the calls."

"I won't argue that."

After they finished eating Clint cleaned the pans and tin plates, made another pot of coffee. They sat together on the same side of the fire so they wouldn't be tempted to look into it.

"Should we set a watch?" Roper asked.

"I suppose so," Clint said. "Somebody might be on our trail for the ransom."

"Speaking of which," Roper said, "where is the ransom?"

"We'll be picking it up in Trinidad."

"How much?"

Clint hesitated.

"That's okay," Roper said. "You don't have to tell me if you don't—"

"A hundred thousand."

Roper whistled.

"You think the Bank of Trinidad will have that much?" he asked.

"Arrangements are being made," Clint said. "They'll have it."

"Then if anybody's following us for the money they'll be real disappointed."

"Yeah," Clint said, "but they won't know that until they've killed us and searched us."

"How comforting."

"I'll take the first watch," Clint said.

"You sure?"

"Yeah," Clint said. "If I remember correctly, I wake up better in the morning than you do."

"You're probably right about that." He dumped the remnants of his coffee onto the ground and stood up. "I'll turn in, then."

"I'll wake you in four hours."

"One question," Roper said. "I find sometimes if you don't ask, you never know."

"Go ahead."

"Do you have any reason to suspect that someone might actually be following us?"

"No," Clint said, "but the two men I encountered in Springfield?"

"Wyatt and Colonel Wentworth?"

Clint nodded.

"I got a telegram from Detective Kingman," Clint said. "He said when he went to talk to them, they were gone."

"Gone," Roper said. "So they could be on our trail."

"Or ahead of us," Clint said. "Or already in Segundo, waiting."

"If they went directly there while you stopped off in Denver."

Clint nodded.

"I get it," Roper said. "If you don't mind, I'll sleep lightly."

"Is there any other way?"

TWENTY-FOUR

Edward Gately was eight years old when the Civil War ended. But he remembered things. He remembered how his mother cried when they got word that his father had been killed by Union soldiers at the first Battle of Bull Run, when he was four. He recalled how she cried again when they heard that his uncle had died at Appomattox, when he was seven. And when he was eight, she cried again when they heard that General Lee had surrendered.

But two years later, when his mother died, he did not cry. And he had not shed a tear since. But he swore by all that was holy that he would do whatever it took to help bring the Confederacy back.

And now he was going to have his chance.

He had been a member of many groups and gangs of disgruntled ex-Confederate soldiers and younger sympathizers like himself, but it wasn't until he met Colonel Wentworth that he found a man he felt was truly worth of following.

Now he waited in Segundo with his own band of men, in command until the Colonel arrived. How he would have flourished in war, he knew, for he was flourishing now beneath the mantle of command.

He went to the window of his hotel room and looked out.

"Eddie," the woman on the bed said.

He didn't answer.

"Eddie!" she said, more stridently.

"Shut up, Katy," he said. "When I want you to open your mouth I'll stick something in it."

"Well come on, then."

He turned and looked at her. She was naked on the bed, lying on her belly with her knees bent, the soles of her feet toward the ceiling. Her bare butt was round and firm, and inviting, but at the moment she was opening her mouth and sticking her tongue out at him.

"Come on," she said, "stick it in. I'll suck on it. You know I will."

Gately was naked, and facing the window as he was she couldn't see that her dirty talk was doing its job. His cock was getting harder.

"Katy," he said, "you have such a filthy mouth."

"I know," she said. "That's why they call me Dirty Katy. It ain't 'cause my snatch is dirty, 'cause it ain't. It's like heaven. Any man I ever been with will tell you that. Nope, it's my mouth." She ran her tongue over her lips. "Come and find out."

He didn't have to find out, though. He already knew. She had awakened him by sucking him dry.

"Come on, Eddie."

He turned back to the window.

"Be quiet, Katy."

"You brought me up here to fuck," she complained, "and I ain't fucked out yet."

She got off the bed, padded naked to the window to stand next to him.

"What's so interesting out there on the street?" she demanded.

"I'm waiting for somebody."

"More interesting than me?" she asked.

He didn't answer.

"More interesting than this?" she asked. She reached down and took his semi-erect cock in her hand, began to stroke him. "Ah, I see you ain't fucked out yet, either, are you?"

Gately looked at her. She wasn't pretty, but the first time he laid eyes on her one word popped into his mind: wanton. He turned out to be correct.

"Katy," he said, "it may be time for you to open that dirty mouth of yours."

"Yes, sir!" she said.

She got down on her knees as he turned to face her, stroked his cock until it was hard, and then opened her mouth so he could stick it in... and out... and in... and out...

***

Later, while Katy dozed, Gately went back to the window to look out. He saw some of his men on the street, wearing their gray coats and kepis, but told not to look for trouble. Others were staying inside, still others were on watch at both ends of town.

Segundo had no law. He knew he and his men could take the town if they wanted to. They'd have to deal with the law in Trinidad, but somebody would have to get there to alert them. They could take the town and bottle everyone up in it, and just wait. His men were growing anxious, eager for some kind of action.

But the call for action was not his to make. He had been in command until only recently, when Wentworth and Wyatt had arrived from Springfield. Now he was second-in-command—third if Wyatt had his way, but the big man would not have his way. It was not his decision to make.

He turned and looked at the girl, who was lying asleep, the sheets on the floor so he could see her naked body. She was on her back, breasts flattened, legs splayed so he could see her dark bush. He felt himself stir again, but it was time to get dressed.

He looked around for his britches...

TWENTY-FIVE

They circled around Colorado Springs. It occurred to Clint that rather than follow them or wait for them in Segundo or even Trinidad, men after the ransom money might wait in Colorado Springs, expecting them to ride through.

"You don't really think anyone expects you to ride all this way carrying a hundred thousand dollars, do you?"

"Why not?" Clint asked. "It'd fit in saddlebags."

"That would mean they'd think we're both carrying them," Roper said. "We've got targets on our backs."

"It wasn't my intention to paint a target on you, Tal," Clint said. "If you want to head back to Denver I wouldn't blame you."

"Hell, no," Roper said. "This little job has piqued my interest, now. Besides, if we get the body back and save the ransom, maybe the government would see fit to give me a finder's fee."

"Well," Clint said, "that's certainly a suggestion I'll make to them."

After they rode a ways in silence Roper spoke again.

"If we had stopped in Colorado Springs, you could have sent a telegram to Washington, let them know where you are."

"That's true."

"So how will they know that you're still on the job

and not dead?"

"If you hired me for a job, what would you think?"

"That you'd get it done," Roper said, "but I know you."

"Well, they know my reputation."

"Aren't you the one who always says reputations are overblown?"

"I do, and I believe it," Clint said. "But that doesn't keep people from believing them. But they didn't hire me blind. They know Jeremy Pike, and Pike knows me. He can vouch for me."

"I don't know if there's a telegraph office between here and Trinidad—or if there's one in Trinidad, for that matter."

"There better be one there," Clint said, "or the money won't be."

"Well," Roper said, "we could try to get the body back without paying."

"Yeah, we could try that."

"You and me," Roper said, "against how many Gray-backs?"

"Who knows?"

"Well, we've got something they don't."

"Oh? What's that?"

Roper looked at him.

"I was hoping you'd agree and tell me."

***

They camped again that night. This time Roper made the coffee, cooked some beans and bacon.

"We'll make Trinidad tomorrow, most likely," he said, "as long as nothing holds us up. We've been push-ing pretty hard."

"Can your horse take it?" Clint asked.

"He'll take it." He washed down a mouthful of bacon and beans with coffee.

"When we pick up that money we will have targets on our backs, for sure," Clint said.

"It's fourteen, maybe fifteen miles to Segundo," Roper said. "We should be able to make it."

"Yeah, but we're not just going to ride in. Not with them waiting for us."

"What's the plan, then?"

"Well, I'm thinking I'll ride in while you stay hidden with the money."

"You're going to trust me with a hundred thousand dollars of the government's money?"

"If I can't trust you, who can I trust?"

"I don't know if I want to be thought of as that trustworthy," Roper said. "I mean, a hundred thousand, that's enough to tempt any man."

"You want to split it fifty-fifty and go our separate way?" Clint asked.

"Fifty grand each?" Roper shook his head. "I'm afraid that's not my price."

"Well then," Clint said, "we'll find out if a hundred grand is your price, won't we, when I leave you alone with it."

"And what if you don't come back?"

"Why would they kill me before they have the money?"

"They're Graybacks," Roper said, "clinging to a dead way of life. That means they're not too smart to begin with."

"If Wentworth is there, he won't let them kill me," Clint said. "I'll want to see Lincoln's body before I pay up. They'd have to expect that."

"They'll show you a casket."

"Uh-uh," Clint said. "They've got to open it."

"Could be anybody in there, by now."

"He might be recognizable."

"What if he's not?"

Clint thought a moment, then said, "I don't know. Don't know what I'd do if I couldn't tell if it was him or not."

"Of course," Roper said, "you could take back any body in a box and say it's him."

"And keep the money, you mean?"

"No," Roper said, "just bring back a body and the money, say it's him, and be done with it. Not have to deal with a bunch of crazy Rebs."

"That's an idea," Clint said, "I think I'll sleep on."

TWENTY-SIX

Roper woke Clint the next morning and handed him a cup of coffee. Clint quickly got to his feet and sipped it.

"You're right," Roper said. "You do wake up better than I do. How do you do that?"

"Like you said, sleep lightly," Clint said, "and I've camped alone on the trail often enough to know that I better wake up ready for anything."

"We better get started if we want to make Trinidad today," Roper said.

"Today, tomorrow," Clint said. "Probably doesn't make that much of a difference. The important thing is that we're there when the bank is open."

"And that the money is there."

"Exactly."

They doused the fire, broke camp, mounted up, and rode.

***

As it turned out they needed to camp one more night on the trail, and they made Trinidad by noon the following day—plenty of time to stop by the bank.

"No matter what happens," Clint said, "we're going to spend the night here, get cleaned up, have a meal."

"Pick up the money?"

"We'll go to the bank," Clint said, "make sure the money's available, and then pick it up tomorrow morning before we go to Segundo."

"Okay, so then a hotel right now?"

"I think if you want to go and get us rooms at the hotel, I'll stop in and see who the law is here."

"I'll go along with you," Roper said. "I'm curious about that myself."

"Fine."

Clint had been to Trinidad during the time Bat Masterson had been the law, so he knew where the sheriff's office was.

They reined in their horses in front of the office and dismounted. Clint grounded Eclipse's reins, while Roper wrapped his horse's reins around the hitching post. They mounted the boardwalk and knocked on the door.

"Yeah, come in!" a voice called.

They opened the door and entered.

"You gotta be strangers, 'cause nobody else in this damn blasted town knocks," a man said. He was coming out from the cell block carrying a worn out broom. The star on his chest looked about as old as the broom, and so did the man. He had lots of gray hair that seemed to be flying all over the place and an unruly gray beard.

"What can I do for ya?" he asked.

"Are you the sheriff?" Clint asked.

"That's me," he said. "Sheriff Rance Harlan, mainly 'cause nobody else wants the job."

"The town looks like it's growing," Roper said. "We saw some new building on the way in, and a nice looking bank."

"The town's fine," the man said, "it's everythin' around us that's gone to hell." The lawman narrowed his eyes at them. "You ain't interested in robbin' the bank, are ya?"

"Not at all," Clint said, "but we do have business there."

Now the sheriff pointed at them.

"Would you be the fellers gonna pick up a hundred thousand dollars?"

Clint and Roper exchanged a glance.

"And how many people in town know about that?" Clint asked.

"Just about everybody," the lawman said. "No secrets here. You wanna head over there now and collect? I'll go with ya."

"We want to go over and make sure the money's available," Clint said. "Then we want a drink, a room, a good meal, and we'll pick the money up in the morning."

"Sounds like a plan," Harlan said. "You wanna tell me what the money is for?"

"No," Clint said.

"Suit yerself, then," Harlan said. "Jest come and get me when you're ready to go to the bank. I'll be yer armed guard."

"Do you wear a gun?" Roper asked, since the man was unarmed.

"Sonny, I was wearin' and usin' a gun before you was off your Momma's teat," the lawman said. "Don't you worry about me. I said I had this job 'cause nobody else wanted it. I didn't say I couldn't do it."

"No offense meant," Roper said.

"No o-ffense taken," Sheriff Harlan said. "You fellers fancy a good steak, place right across the street's got the best in town."

"Thanks," Clint said, "we'll try it."

"And try the Trinidad Inn for rooms," Harlan went

on. "Used to be called the Trinidad House. Personally, I think that sounded better, but ain't my decision."

"Thank you, Sheriff," Clint said. "We'll see you tomorrow."

"And don't be gettin' into no trouble while yer here," the lawman said. "I keep a nice quiet town."

"Do you want our names?" Roper asked.

Harlan held up his hand. "No names, thanks. That'd probably only make me worry. Just watch yer P's and Q's."

"Gotcha," Clint said. "Thanks for your time."

The two friends left the office and stopped outside.

"Not what I expected," Roper said.

"Maybe not," Clint said, "but I bet he can do the job."

"Yeah," Roper said, "that's the feeling I got."

"Come on," Clint said. "We'll see to the horses, get rooms, and then eat."

"Suits me."

They picked up their reins and walked their animals over to the livery.

TWENTY-SEVEN

As Clint and Roper rode into town they attracted the attention of the townspeople—and now they knew why. Everybody knew about the money.

Another man who knew about the money was sitting in a chair across the street from the sheriff's office, whittling. When Clint and Roper left and went to the livery, he folded his knife, pocketed his wood, and walked across.

As he entered the office he said, "Was that them?"

"There ya go," the lawman said, "that's more like it, folks just bustin' in here without knockin'."

"Was that them?"

"Was that who?"

"The fellas who are gonna be pickin' up the money."

The sheriff narrowed his eyes.

"Now Jason, don't you go be lookin' for no trouble."

"That's a lot of money, Sheriff."

"What the hell would you do with that much money, you danged fool?" Harlan asked. "Yeah, that was them."

"When are they pickin' it up?"

"Tomorrow mornin'," Harlan said, "and I'll be with 'em."

"Okay, okay," Jason said. "Simmer down, Sheriff. Don't get all hot under the collar."

"If you and your kind aim to take that money off'n them, you better wait until their outta town, ya hear?"

121

"I hear, Sheriff," Jason said, "I hear. Any idea what they need the money for?"

"No idee at all," the lawman said, "and I don't care a plugged nickel."

"Okay," Jason said, "sorry for botherin' ya, Sheriff."

"Danged fools," Harlan muttered, grabbing his broom, "the lot of 'em."

Jason left the office and stopped just outside the door. He looked up and down the street, didn't see the two men anywhere. He assumed they were in the livery stable, which was fine with him.

He stepped into the street and crossed over, turned, and headed for the Nickel & Dime Saloon.

***

In his office, Sheriff Harlan took a couple of disgruntled swipes at the floor with his broom, then set it aside and rubbed his face with both hands. There was going to be trouble for sure, damn it. He went to his desk, opened a drawer, took out his gunbelt, and strapped it on.

TWENTY-EIGHT

Clint and Roper checked into separate rooms, and then went to check out the place the sheriff had suggested for a steak.

The restaurant had a board over the doorway with one name on it, BETSY'S, but the windows had BETSY'S STEAKHOUSE printed on them, on either side of the door.

As they entered a man approached and said, "Sit anywhere, gents. We're kinda between meals at the moment."

It was true. It was between lunch and dinner, so the place was fairly empty, except for one other table, where a man sat eating.

They grabbed a table against the back wall, where nobody could get behind them but they could see the front door.

"What kin I get for you boys?" the waiter asked. "Just passin' through?"

"We are," Clint said. "Two steak dinners, if we can get them this early."

"You can get whatever ya want," the man said. "Steaks comin' up. Beers?"

"Please," Roper said.

"Right away."

Both men had taken the time to clean off the trail

dust while in their rooms, but they still needed to wash the dust from their throats.

"So," Roper said, "no secret why we're in town."

"I suppose not."

"A hundred thousand is a big temptation," Roper said. "Somebody's going to make a try for it—and maybe more than one somebody."

"We'll be ready," Clint said.

"Now I know how men feel when they're transporting a payroll," Roper said.

"Never did a payroll delivery job?"

"Can't say I have."

"I've done it once or twice," Clint said. "Mostly quiet work. Just once in a while somebody gets a big idea."

"Well, somebody's going to get a big idea here," Roper said. "And it may not be somebody from this town."

"I know," Clint said. "I thought about that. Some Graybacks may decide they're not such believers in the cause—not when there's a hundred thousand on the line."

"Well, I'm glad you're covering all the angles," Roper said.

"When have you ever known me not to?"

"True."

The waiter came with big frosty mugs of beer.

"Steaks are almost ready, gents."

"Onions?" Roper asked.

"Plenty of them."

"Yes!"

"Don't think I've ever had a bad steak," Roper said. "Bloody or burnt, I'll eat it."

Clint didn't respond. He was deep in thought.

"Clint? Where are you?"

"Huh? Oh, sorry," Clint said. "Just thinking about

tomorrow."

"What were you thinking?"

"Maybe you should stay behind."

"Why?"

"Well, if we're not hit on the way to Segundo, then I'm going to leave you alone to ride in. That leaves you vulnerable."

"And it leaves you vulnerable in town," Roper said.

"Yeah, but you'll have the money."

"Then maybe we should ride in together."

"With the money?"

"No," Roper said. "We do that and they'll just take the money and do whatever they want with Lincoln."

"I agree."

"We could bury the money somewhere," Roper said, "once we're sure we're not being watched."

Clint considered the option.

"That would mean neither one of us would have to go it alone," he said.

"Right," Roper said, "we could die together."

At that moment the waiter came with their steaks and set the plates down.

"Why don't we wait to talk about dying after we eat?" Clint suggested.

"Good point."

***

After they finished their excellent steaks they left the restaurant and walked over to the bank. Clint presented himself, not to a teller, but to a pretty lady seated at a desk.

"I'd like to see the manager, please."

"Of course," she said. "May I tell him your name and

your business?"

"Yes," Clint said. "My name is Clint Adams, and I think he'll know my business."

"Oh, of course!" she said. Obviously, she knew his business. "I'll just be a minute."

The bank was one of the new buildings in Town Roper had mentioned to the sheriff. It even smelled like new wood.

The lady came back and said, "Gentlemen, would you follow me, please?"

She led them to an office, stepped aside so they could enter.

"The manager is Mr. Dwight."

"Thank you," Clint said.

He and Roper entered, and a tall, lean man in his forties stood up from behind his desk, smoothing down his tie. It was difficult for the man to hide his nervousness.

"Mr. Adams?" he said.

"That's right," Clint said, shaking the man's hand. "This is my colleague, Mr. Talbot Roper."

Dwight shook hands with Roper, looking at him quizzically.

"He is a private detective from Denver, and a friend of mine," Clint said. "He's going to accompany me to deliver the ransom."

"I'm going to keep him from getting killed while he does it," Roper said.

"Of course, of course," Mr. Dwight said. "Please, gentlemen, sit."

They each took a seat.

"I assume there's no problem?" Clint said. "The money is here?"

"The money is indeed here. You have a letter of introduction, of course?"

"Of course." Clint took it out and handed it over. It was one of the things he found in his hotel room in Washington. It was signed by the President of the United States. The bank manager handed it back nervously, as if handling a piece of paper bearing such an august name shattered his nerves.

"W-would you be wanting the money now?" he asked.

"No," Clint said, "we'll be coming back early tomorrow morning with the sheriff to pick up the money. I just wanted to make sure there would be no problems."

"None that I can foresee," the bank manager said. "Would you be wanting any kind of escort? To your horses? Or further?"

"No," Clint said, "that won't be necessary. The sheriff can see us to our horses. After that we'll be on our own."

"Very well, then," Dwight said. "Is there anything else I—I can do for you?" He rubbed his hands together, but not before Clint could see the moisture on them. He'd also felt it when he shook hands with the man.

"You can tell me what's making you so nervous, Mr. Dwight," Clint said.

"Nervous?" the man asked. "D-do I seem nervous?"

"You're stammering," Roper said, "and your hands are clammy."

"And your glasses are steaming up," Clint point out.

The man took off his wire-framed glasses and looked at them.

"Yes, well," he said, taking out a handkerchief to wipe them with, "this is a great deal of money we have in the bank, m-more than usual, and y-you are... well, who you are."

"It makes you this nervous that he's the Gunsmith?" Roper asked.

"Well... yes." He put his glasses back on in an extremely fussy manner, making sure they sat just so on his nose. "I mean, given his r-reputation, and a-all."

"And that's all?" Clint asked. "That's it?"

"C-certainly," Dwight said. "What else could there be?"

"Well," Roper said, "just off the top of my head, you wouldn't by any chance be planning to have anyone try to relieve us of this money, would you?"

"What?" The man seemed shocked. "N-no, not at all! I—this is m-my bank. I would never—"

"Okay, okay,' Clint said. "Relax. Mr. Roper was just asking. After all, we do expect someone to try and steal this money."

"Y-you do?" the man asked.

"Of course," Clint said. "Like you said, it's a lot of money."

"Yes, b-but—"

"Relax, Mr. Dwight," Clint said, standing. "We'll get out of your hair now."

Roper stood. "We'll see you in the morning, bright and early."

"Please have the money ready," Clint said.

"Oh, yes, sir," Dwight said, "of course."

Roper smiled at the man and said, "Have a nice day."

TWENTY-NINE

"**D**id you believe him?" Roper asked, outside.

"He seems to be a fussy man," Clint said. "I'd believe that his hands are always clammy. And could you see him directing men to come after us?"

"Okay," Roper said, "what if he's nervous because he's being coerced into helping somebody steal the money?"

"Why would they wait until we get here to get the manager of the bank to help them?" Clint asked. "They could get him to open the back door and the vault at night."

"And the fact that they haven't..."

":... means that he probably can't be bought."

"Okay," Roper said, "so we just have to get from the front door to our horses." He pointed.

"Or go out the back."

Roper thought about that for a moment, then shook his head.

"No," he said, "but we can make somebody think we're going out the back."

"How?"

"Have horses waiting out there," Roper said.

"People know my horse."

"Pack horses," Roper went on. "Put a couple of pack horses back there, make them think we're going out that

129

way with the money. Or that one of us is."

"Then we make a dash out the front, mount up and ride."

"Sounds good to me," Roper said.

"Time for a drink?"

"Is that smart?" Roper said. "Going into a saloon?"

"Who's going to hit us before we have the money?" Clint asked.

"Good point. I could use another beer."

They stepped off the boardwalk and walked across the street toward a saloon called the Nickel & Dime.

***

Jason Tucker saw Clint Adams and another man enter the saloon, reached out, and touched his partner's arm.

"There they are," he said.

Victor Coleman looked at them over his mug of beer.

"Who's the other fella?"

"I don't know."

"You sure that's Adams?"

"Yeah."

"How?"

"I seen him before, a few years ago."

"How'd you know they'd come in here?"

"The bank's right across the street."

Victor nodded.

"So what do we do?"

"We watch."

"Why don't we take 'em?"

"You think they got a hundred thousand dollars in their pockets?"

"Oh."

"Yeah, oh," Jason said. "Don't try to think, Vic. Just

do what I say."

"What about the others?"

"I'll get to them," Jason said. "As soon as we find out when and how they intend to get to the money."

"You think your contact in the bank will come through?"

Jason smiled.

"She'll come through if she ever wants to get fucked again," he said. "I'm tellin' you, this girl never had it before, and now she can't get enough. Oh yeah, she'll talk to me."

"When?"

"Tonight."

"So what do we do 'til then?"

"Watch," Jason said, "and drink your beer."

THIRTY

Clint and Roper each ordered a beer.

"Eyes on us?" Clint asked.

"Oh, yeah," Roper said, "but like you said, they won't try anything until we have the money."

'Let's talk to the sheriff about having pack horses at the back door of the bank."

"Can we trust him?"

"He's the one person we're going to take a chance on," Clint said. "And then he can have somebody take the horses to the back door."

"Okay," Roper said. "We might as well drink these down and get that done."

They finished their beers and walked out, seemingly without looking around.

***

"They're oblivious," Jason said.

"Huh?" Victor said.

"They don't know what's going on around them," Jason said. "This should be easy."

"Easy?" Victor said. "That's the Gunsmith."

"This is not the old west anymore, Victor," Jason said. "His time has passed. It's our time, now."

"Jason," Victor said, "I don't think—"

"That's the first smart thing you've said today," Jason said. "Don't think."

***

"You want to put two horses at the back door of the bank?" the sheriff said.

"Pack horses," Clint said.

"No saddles."

"We want it to look like we're going to put the money on the pack horses."

Sheriff Harlan sat back in his chair and regarded the two men.

"Sounds like a good plan," he said, finally. "If anybody's lookin' to hit you for that money they'd be waitin' at the back door."

"We hope," Roper said.

"But," Harlan said, "the horses will have to be loaded down. If you're really not takin' them with you, what happens to the supplies?"

"They go back to the store," Clint said.

"It'll still cost," Harlan said.

"We'll pay for the supplies," Clint said, "you see that they get back to the mercantile."

"I can do that," Harlan said. "And I'll have Henry over at the livery put the horses behind the bank."

"Can we trust him?" Clint asked.

"Can you trust me?" Harlan asked.

"I hope so," Clint said.

"Henry's my cousin," Harlan said. "Don't worry about it. What time are you headin' for the bank?"

"Eight a.m.," Clint said.

"I'll see you boys then."

Clint and Roper turned in early. Early the next morning while he was dressing Clint looked out his window and saw the sheriff standing in front of his office, wearing his gun.

"Attaboy, Sherriff."

Then he saw a man walking two loaded pack horses past the hotel.

"Attaboy, Henry," he said.

THIRTY-ONE

lint and Roper met in the hotel lobby and checked out.

"Hope you enjoyed your stay," the clerk said.

"It was better than sleeping on the ground," Roper said, then on the way to the door he added to Clint, "Just barely."

Outside they saw the sheriff crossing the street toward them.

"Henry's got the horses behind the bank," he told them.

"I saw him walking them past the hotel," Clint said.

"And your horses are waiting at the livery, saddled and ready."

"Henry saddled my horse?" Clint asked.

"He's good with horses," Sheriff Harlan said, "and he's missing two fingers, anyway."

"We'll meet you in front of the bank, Sheriff."

The man nodded, and then went their separate ways.

***

"Are you sure about this?" Victor asked Jason.

"I heard it from Henry, over at the livery," Jason said. "They're having him take two pack horses behind the bank."

"But I don't think—"

"I do," Jason said. "Have the other three boys meet behind the saloon. We'll be able to see the back of the bank from there. When they come out, we'll hit them."

"Whatever you say," Victor said.

***

Clint and Roper rode their horses over to the Trinidad bank and dismounted.

"I'll go inside with you," the sheriff said.

"Good," Clint said. He didn't think the lawman was up to anything underhanded, but he was prepared. He knew Roper felt the same way.

The three men entered the bank, which had only been open for about five minutes. The bank manager was waiting, rubbing his hands together nervously.

"Good mornin', Mr. Dwight," Harlan said.

"'Morning, Sheriff."

"These gentlemen are here to pick up their money."

"Yes, sir. Right this way, gentlemen."

He walked Clint and Roper to a teller's cage, while other employees stood around and watched. The man behind the cage looked bored. He also looked like he'd been a teller for fifty years. He'd probably seen hundreds of these transactions.

"Mr. Wardell, would you count out the money for these gents?" Dwight asked.

"Yes, sir."

"And put it all in these saddlebags," Clint said, pushing his and Roper's saddlebags into the teller's cage.

"Yes, sir."

The clerk started his count, banding the money into stacks, and then putting a stack at a time into the saddlebags.

"Evenly distributed between the saddlebags?" he asked.

"That's right," Clint said. He figured he and Roper should carry an equal amount of money.

Clint's saddlebags grew fatter, and then the man started on Roper's. All the while the manager, Dwight, was looking on nervously. The sheriff stood behind Clint and Roper, keeping his eye on the front door.

"All done, Mr. Dwight," the teller said. "We just need the gentlemen to sign."

"Mr. Adams will sign," Dwight said.

The teller pushed a piece of paper to Clint, who signed it and slid it back. The teller than pushed the saddlebags through to Clint, who handed one set to Roper and slung the other set over his shoulder.

"Ready, Sheriff," he said.

"Let's go."

The old lawman walked to the door, opened it, and peered out.

"Looks like it's working," he said. "There may be some nosy folks watching, but nobody's on the street, and I don't see rifles on the rooftops."

"I hope you're right," Clint said.

He looked at Roper. If the entire town got together to take this money off them, there'd be nothing they could do about it. Not against a whole town.

"Don't worry," Harlan said. "The whole town's not gonna try to rob you."

Clint looked at Roper, wondering if Harlan was a mind reader.

"Hey," Roper said, "I'm encouraged."

"Let's just walk out, get on our horses, and ride," Clint said.

Roper nodded.

The sheriff opened the door wide and stepped out first, then to the side. He kept his hand on his gun.

Clint and Roper stepped out, quickly went to the horses, tossed their saddlebags onto their saddles, and mounted up. They'd tie them off when they were away.

"Much obliged, Sheriff," Clint said, giving the lawman a salute.

"Good luck."

Clint and Roper turned their horses and rode out of Trinidad.

***

Behind the saloon, still watching the two packhorses behind the bank, Jason heard horses and said, "What the hell is that?"

THIRTY-TWO

They pushed the horses until they felt they were a safe distance from town, then reined in. They dismounted and tied their saddlebags off.

"Well, that went off without a hitch," Roper said, looking behind them.

"See anybody?" Clint asked.

"No," Roper said. "Nobody, no sign."

"As soon as they realize we fooled them, they'll be coming," Clint said. "We better keep moving."

"Keep running?"

"If we have to turn and fight we will," Clint said, "but there's always a chance they'll give up."

"I suppose."

They mounted up and continued riding south. Segundo was about fourteen miles.

***

When they were outside of Segundo they stopped. Clint stood in his stirrups and looked behind them.

"No sign," he said.

"You seem disappointed."

Clint looked at Roper.

"I'm thinking maybe we should have taken care of this in Trinidad."

"You mean gone out that back door and met it head on?"

"Yeah."

"Well, it's too late to change that decision," Roper said. "Maybe you were right, and they got discouraged."

"I'd say a hundred thousand dollars is whole a lot of encouragement," Clint said.

"We might as well face the problem that's ahead of us rather than worry about the one behind us," Roper said.

"You're right," Clint said. "How much further to Segundo?"

"I think when we top that rise ahead we'll see it."

Clint looked around.

"We need someplace to bury these saddlebags," he said.

Roper did the same as Clint, looking around them for a likely spot.

"How about there?" He pointed to an outcropping of rocks. "We might be able to cover them with rocks instead of actually burying them in the dirt."

"Let's go take a look."

They rode over to the rocks and dismounted.

"Look," Roper said, pointing. "There's a hollowed out area there, perfect for a hiding place."

"First let's see if it's so perfect other people have already used it."

They got on their knees to look inside the hollowed out area.

"Doesn't look like anything's been in there for years," Roper said.

"Except maybe an animal or two," Clint said, pointing to some small tracks.

"Small animals," Roper said. "And once we cover it

no animal will be able to get in. Besides, we're not going to leave the money in there for very long."

"True. Okay, let's see how the saddlebags fit."

They both walked to their horses and grabbed their saddlebags. Clint stuffed his through the opening, then took Roper's and did the same.

"Tight fit," he said.

"All the more reason nothing else will be able to get in," Roper said. "Let's see how well we can cover it up."

They looked around for stones and rocks that were the right size and shape, began to build a small wall in front of the opening. After a while they rose to stand back and take a look.

"How's it look?" Clint asked.

"Not very natural," Roper said, "but a rider could bypass it without a second look."

"Let's put some brush in front of it," Clint suggested.

"Good idea."

They walked around, collecting loose brush, and piled it in front of the rocks, then stood back again.

"That's better," Clint said.

"Yes," Roper said, "a bit."

They both stared at it for a while, then Clint said, "Makes me nervous leaving a hundred thousand dollars out here like this."

"Temporarily," Roper said, "but I understand."

Clint brushed his hands off on his thighs and said, "Well, we'd better get going. The Graybacks are probably getting nervous."

"If, like you say, this Colonel Wentworth is there, then they have an experienced officer to keep them in line."

"He maybe experienced," Clint said, "but I have no idea how good an officer he was."

"I guess that's something we're going to find out."

THIRTY-THREE

The rode into Segundo twenty minutes later.

By the time they did, one of the lookouts had announced the approach of two riders. Edward Gately was out in front of the hotel with six of his men, all wearing Confederate jackets.

"What if it's not them?" Jed Morehouse asked. He was tall, in his thirties, with a corporal's stripes on his arm.

"Then we got set up out here for nothin'," Gately said. "But I think it's them."

"What makes you so sure, Captain?"

Gately looked at his corporal and said, "Because it's time."

Gately looked up the street as the two riders came closer...

***

Clint and Roper saw the seven men waiting for them in front of the hotel.

"Looks like a welcoming committee," Roper said.

"Been a while since I've seen that many gray uniforms," Clint commented.

"Makes me itch." Hartman touched the extra revolver he kept in a holster that was sewn to his saddle.

"Anytime you feel like you have to make a move, make it," Clint told him. "I'll back you."

"Same here."

They rode up to the waiting men and reined in. One man wearing captain's bars stepped down into the street.

"Clint Adams?" he asked.

"That's me?"

"And this gent?"

"Talbot Roper," Roper said.

"A friend of mine."

"You were told to come alone," the captain said.

"No," Clint said, "I wasn't. I was told to bring whatever help I thought I needed."

"One man," one of the other Graybacks said derisively.

"That's all I need," Clint said, looking at the man who wore corporal's stripes. "And you?" he asked, turning his gaze to the captain.

"Captain Edward Gately."

"Captain of what Army?" Clint asked.

"Do not be insulting, sir."

"I'm not here to talk to a man who thinks he's an officer," Clint said.

"Where's the money?" Gately asked.

Clint grinned rightly. "Certainly not on me. I need to speak to your superior... *Captain*."

"I'll demand your respect, sir," Gately said, "if not for me, then for this uniform."

"First of all," Roper said, "you had a runny nose when that actually was a uniform."

The six men behind Gately tensed, and he held a hand out to stay them from any foolish moves.

"I'll talk to Colonel Wentworth," Clint said, "not to you."

"Wentworth?" Gately asked.

"Don't pretend you don't know who he is," Clint said, "or that he's not here."

"No, no," Gately said, "I'll take you to Wentworth. Your friend can stay here with my men."

"I'll come along," Roper said.

Gately looked at Roper, who stared back unwaveringly.

"In that case," he said, "we'll all go."

"Just point the way," Clint said.

"The far end of town," Gately said. "Corporal, three men in front and three in back, please."

"Yes, sir!"

The men stepped down from the boardwalk and took up their positions.

"Are you ready?" Gately asked Clint.

"Ready as we'll ever be."

***

The house stood outside of town a ways, not inside the town limits. It was nothing like Wentworth's house in Springfield. This one was large, taking up one floor, but it was in need of work. They stopped on the outside of the once white fence that surrounded the house.

"You can leave your horses here," Gately said.

Clint and Roper dismounted, Roper using the fence to tie his horse off. As he usually did, Clint simply grounded Eclipse's reins. The Darley Arabian would not go anywhere unless he thought he had to.

Gately led the way to the front door, with three men flanking him. Clint and Roper followed, with the other three men behind them.

When they reached the door Gately stepped to it and

knocked. The door was opened by a black man wearing a white jacket and black tie.

"Suh?" he said to Gately.

"These are the men we've been waitin' for," Gately said. "They want to see the person in charge."

"Yes, sir," the black man said. "Please come in."

"After you gents," Gately said, letting Clint and Roper enter first. He then followed, leaving five of the solders outside and taking only his Corporal with him.

Just inside the door he said, "I'll need your guns."

"What?" Clint asked.

"The only way this works is if we take your guns," Gately said.

"You're kidding," Roper said.

"Not at all."

"Ain't going to happen," Clint said. "We give up our guns, then we're not on equal ground."

"What makes you think you were ever on equal ground from the moment you rode into town?"

"Not giving up our guns," Clint said.

"You will not get the casket if you don't give up your guns."

"And you will not get your money if you try to take them," Clint said.

"Looks like a stalemate," Roper said. "I think you need someone in authority to make this decision for you, son."

Gately's face grew red, but someone else stepped into the entry foyer at that moment, surprising Clint.

"They can keep their guns," she said.

"But Ma'am—"

"Captain," Gemma Wentworth said, "who's in charge here, you or me?"

"You, Ma'am."

"Then they can keep their guns," she said. She looked at Clint and Roper. "Follow me please, gentlemen."

THIRTY-FOUR

They followed Gemma Wentworth into a sparsely furnished living room, where Clint expected to see her husband, Colonel Wentworth.

"Where's your husband?" Clint asked.

"You don't need him," she said. She was wearing a man's shirt, trousers and boots, a far cry from the dress she wore in Springfield.

"What are you talking about?" Clint said. "You know why I'm here. We need to negotiate—"

"You negotiate with me, Clint." She folded her arms across her chest.

"You?"

"I'm in charge," she said. "Are you surprised?"

"Well, yes."

Roper certainly was.

"When did this happen?" Clint asked.

"I've been in charge all along," she said. "Even back in Springfield."

Now Clint *was* surprised.

"I'm sorry," she said. "I couldn't tell you then. But everything that we... everything that happened was... needed."

Clint looked at Roper, who was staring at the woman.

"Where's the money?" she asked.

"Where's the President?"

"You mean Lincoln's body?" she asked. "He's certainly not the President anymore."

"He'll always be The President to me."

"Well, that's your problem," she said. "The fact is he's a cold, long dead corpse."

"Worth a hundred thousand dollars."

"That," she said, "was my husband's idea. I think he's worth more."

"We didn't bring more," Clint said.

"Oh, I know that," she said. "No, no, we'll stick to the original bargain. Just tell us where the money is."

"Show us the casket first."

"I'm sorry," she said, "but that doesn't work for me."

"Then we're at an impasse," he said.

"No," she said, "we can work something out. Are you hungry?"

"I am," Roper admitted.

"Yes," Clint said, "we're hungry."

"Simon," she said to the black man, "lay out some food for our friends."

"Yes, Ma'am."

"We'll talk—negotiate—over some food," she told Clint. "Edward, you will join us."

"Yes, Ma'am."

"And what about the Colonel?"

"Don't worry about my husband," she said. "He'll be around. Just have a seat here and wait. I will go and change so we can eat."

"Ma'am?" Gately said.

"You wait with them, Captain," she said. "The Corporal can leave, unless you think you need him. But he will not be eating with us."

"Yes, Ma'am."

She left the room, presumably to go to her bedroom

and change clothes. Clint wondered where Samuel Wentworth was.

Clint and Roper both sat down on the sofa.

"Have a seat, Captain," Clint said. "Like the lady said, we'll just wait to eat."

"Do you think you need your corporal?" Roper asked. "To keep you safe?"

Gately's face grew red.

"Corporal, you can go," he said.

"But, sir."

"I'll call you when I need you," Gately said. "Wait outside with the rest of the men."

"Yes, sir."

The corporal left, and Gately sat in an armchair that had seen better days.

After a little bit of time had gone by with no one speaking, Clint broke the silence.

"What's going on, Captain?" Clint asked.

"What do you mean?"

"Where's the Colonel?"

"The Colonel has been having some... problems for a long time," the young captain said. "That is why Mrs. Wentworth stepped up to take over."

"Really?" Roper asked. "Aren't you second-in-command, Captain?"

"I am second-in-command here," Gately said, "of this division. She is in command of—"

"Captain?"

The black man Simon had entered the room.

"Yes?"

"Lunch is served."

"Keep it hot until Mrs. Wentworth returns."

"Yes, sir."

Simon went back into the kitchen.

"Where is he, Captain?" Clint asked. "Where's the Colonel?"

"It won't be necessary to answer that, Captain," Gemma said, reappearing. She was wearing a long, high-necked dress. "It's time to eat."

THIRTY-FIVE

The lunch was more sumptuous than most dinners. Clint wondered where this band of ex-Confederates got their supplies from.

Gemma did most of the talking, and most of it was about a reborn Confederacy. It sounded like she was espousing her husband's dream, but from the look on her face she believed every word of it.

"Back when there was a Confederacy," she said, "we lived in a beautiful house in Virginia. We had servants, slaves, friends... we had a life. Good wine, good food, elegant clothes... and then the Union came. They burned it all, while Samuel was away at the war. They came and burned us out. So you see, they owe us. The owe me!" Her eyes blazed.

"So for those reasons you steal President Lincoln's body," Clint said.

"Wyatt came to Samuel with the idea. My husband went for it. He said the money would go into our war chest." She looked at Captain Gately. "Captain, why don't you take Mr. Roper out for some air. Right out back."

"I got men out front, Ma'am—"

"Out back will be fine." She obviously wanted to talk to Clint alone.

Roper looked at Clint, who nodded. The captain and

Roper both got up and went out the back door.

"Simon," Gemma said, "give us a few minutes."

"Yes, Ma'am."

"Take the Colonel some food."

"Yes, Ma'am."

Simon made a tray up and left the kitchen with it.

Gemma reached across the table and put her hand on Clint's arm.

"After this payment we'll have a half-a-million in our war chest," she said. "Samuel thinks that will buy back the Confederacy."

"And you don't?"

'The South is dead," she said. "It was dead the minute Lee surrendered. Men like my husband have been fooling themselves for years."

"But not you, huh?"

"No, not me," she said.

"So that money's yours?" he asked. "How you going to get it away from the Captain and his men?"

"The Captain is a young man who has never been to war," she said. "He can be bought."

"With money?"

She smiled. "And other things."

"Ah. You think he'll go for that?"

"I don't know," she said. "I'm not quite past my prime yet. Maybe he will. Or maybe I'll need some help."

"From me?"

"Half-a-million dollars, Clint," she said. "Think about it. We were good together in Springfield."

"That was one night, Gemma."

"We could be good again."

He slid his arm away from her touch.

"I don't think so," he said. "I'm here to do a job. You see, my side won the war. We're still around."

She drew her hand back and sneered. "Bluebellies. How do I know you weren't there the day they burned me out?"

"You don't," he said. "I don't. If I was there we were both pretty young."

"It doesn't matter," she said. "I still remember it very well."

"Well, I don't."

"How many plantations did you burn, Clint, that you don't remember anymore?"

"That wasn't my job," he said. "But this is. Have your young captain take me to Lincoln's body."

She sat back in her chair and composed herself. Through the window on the door Clint could see Roper and Gately standing outside. They were not talking. In fact, they weren't even looking at each other.

"Tomorrow," she said, finally. "Take the night. Sleep on my offer."

"I don't think so, Gemma," Clint said. "I don't think I want to sleep in this town. Take us to the body and we'll get you the money and be on our way."

"Get me half the money," she said, "and I'll show you where the body is."

Clint looked out the window again. Suddenly, there were three more gray uniforms back there, and they were all pointing guns at Roper who, in turn, was pointing his gun at Gately.

"We'll keep your friend here until you get back."

Clint drew his gun and pointed it at Gemma, who reared back, looking surprised.

"Roper and I will go and get half the money and come back," he said. "Have the Captain bring him back in here."

"And if I don't?"

"I'll kill you right now, Gemma."

"You wouldn't," she said. "How would you get the body back, then?"

He cocked the hammer on his gun and said, "That's not something you're going to have to worry about."

THIRTY-SIX

emma stared at the gun and for a moment Clint thought she was going to be brave enough to try to call what she thought was his bluff, but in the end she stood, walked to the door and said, "Captain, bring Mr. Roper inside, please."

Clint heard Gately say, "Yes, ma'am," and he and Roper reentered the kitchen. They both saw Clint's gun in his hand.

"What's gong on?" Gately asked.

"Change of plan," Gemma said. "Mr. Adams and Mr. Roper will go and get half the money and bring it to us. We will then take them to the casket."

"Along with the wagon that was used to transport it here," Clint said.

"Our wagon?" she asked.

"We'll buy it from you."

She nodded. "Very well."

Clint stood up and holstered his gun.

"There's going to be a mess out front if your soldiers go for their guns when we step out," he said.

"The Captain will escort you to your horses."

"Yes, Ma'am."

The Captain left the kitchen, followed by Roper. As Clint started to follow, Gemma put her hand on his left arm.

"You wouldn't have really shot me, would you?" she asked.

"To save my friend?" he said. "In a second."

She took her hand away and he followed the other two men.

***

As they went out the front door the six soldiers came to attention. Clint noticed for the first time how their uniform jackets had been mended and tended to, over and over. The Captain's jacket, however, was impeccable.

"You know the deal," Gately said. "Half the money."

"We know the deal, Captain," Clint said. "And if anyone should try to follow us, it wouldn't end well."

"Understood."

Clint and Roper mounted up and rode back up the street the way they had come.

***

"We just gonna let them go?" Corporal Morehouse asked.

"That's right," Gately said.

"But... why?"

"Because, Corporal," Gately said, "those are our orders."

"B-but—"

"They'll be right back with half of the money."

"Half?" Morehouse said. "What if they just ride off with all of it? Shouldn't we go with them?"

"No, we shouldn't," Gately said. "They'll be back."

"How can you be sure?"

"They want their dead President."

"Jesus," Morehouse said, "it's just a damn corpse—

and an old one, at that."

"That's Union thinking for you," Captain Gately said. He turned and went back into the house.

***

Gemma Wentworth was sitting on the sofa in the living room.

"Are they gone?"

"Yes, Ma'am."

Simon entered the room with an empty tray.

"Did he eat?"

"Yes, Ma'am."

"Good," she said. "You can clean the kitchen now."

"Yes, Ma'am."

"And how are you doing, Captain?"

"Fine, Ma'am."

"And your whore? What's her name?"

"Katy."

"Is she keeping you happy?"

"Yes, Ma'am."

"Come closer, Captain."

He took a few steps, so he was within her reach. She unbuttoned his trousers, reached inside and took out his cock. It was already beginning to swell, and got harder still as she stroked it.

"Is she really? Look at that. That doesn't look like it's been taken care of, does it?"

"No, Ma'am," he said.

"Oh yeah," she said, "there it is, nice and big. Look at that. I'll bet that keeps her happy, doesn't it?"

"Yes, Ma'am."

She leaned forward so that her mouth was very close to the head of his penis, then looked up at him and said,

"You don't mind, do you?"

"No, Ma'am."

She smiled at him, then opened her mouth and practically swallowed him whole...

***

"Nobody following," Roper said.

"I didn't think they would," Clint said.

"What was that about in the kitchen?"

"What was that about outside?"

"Suddenly I was surrounded by gray coats, and they wanted my gun," Roper said.

"Well, I told her they had to let you go or I'd shoot her."

"Obviously, it worked."

"Yes."

"You know they're going to try and keep the body after we give them the money, don't you? That woman is crazy."

"I know," Clint said. "I thought of that."

"That means gunplay."

"Yup."

"That's a ragtag looking lot of soldiers."

"Those six, anyway," Clint said. "Who knows how many others there are."

"I think we're going to find that out the hard way," Roper said.

***

Gemma finished with Captain Gately and sucking his penis dry, stowing the thing back in his pants and then giving his crotch one last pat. She sat back and wiped the corners of her mouth with her fingertips.

"That was very sweet, Captain. Thank you. Now you'd better go back outside and watch for our friends to return," she said.

"Yes, Ma'am."

"And have the rest of the men ready," she said, "for when we take them to the casket."

"Are we actually gonna give it to them?"

"No," she said, "but we're going to take them to it so they can see what they're not getting."

"And then we kill them?"

"I haven't decided yet," she said. "I may keep them alive to bring us more money."

"Do you think the government would send more money?" Gately asked.

"If they want their dear Mr. Lincoln's remains back they will."

"But... are we ever gonna really send it back?"

"No, my dear, sweet Captain," she said, "we're going to have a great big bonfire with it when we're done. How does that strike you?"

"That strikes me just fine, Ma'am," Gately said. "And, uh, the Colonel?"

"Don't you worry about the Colonel, Captain," she said. "Just trust that he is in my very good care."

"Yes, Ma'am."

"Now, off you go, you sweet, boy. And don't waste all that sweetness on your whore. I may be wanting some more of it myself."

"Yes, Ma'am."

THIRTY-SEVEN

When Clint and Roper reached the rocks where they had hidden the money they reined their horses in and waited, looking around.

"Nobody followed from town," Roper said.

"I'm surprised," Clint said.

"Why?" Roper asked. "They know we're bringing the money in."

"Half the money," Clint said. "The only way they get the other half is to give us the casket."

"Which they will then try to take back again, no doubt," Roper said.

"We'll deal with that when the time comes," Clint said. "Right now we need to dig up half that money." He dismounted. "You keep watch while I do that."

"Got it."

Clint uncovered the saddlebags, removed one set, and then covered the other one up again while Roper kept watch so nobody could sneak up on them. When he was done he tied the saddlebags to his saddle and remounted.

"Let's get back," he said.

Carefully studying their surroundings, they directed their horses back to Segundo.

***

Captain Gately sat in a chair in front of the hotel while he and his men waited for Clint and Roper to return. His legs felt weak from what Gemma had done to his cock while he was in the house with her. Not that he minded. The woman really knew what she was doing, and she was fine looking. And the closer he got to her, the closer he got to being in command. It was clear that Gemma was cutting her husband out of the picture, which suited Gately.

He had several of his soldiers on his side of the street, still more on the other side. And there was a detachment of men staying with the casket. The only way Clint Adams and Talbot Roper would leave town with the dead President was if Gately and his men let them—and they would, only to take it back somewhere on the trail.

"And," Gemma had told him, "if it's at all possible, kill them while you're at it—and then come back here and tell me all about it."

"Yes, Ma'am."

"And then we'll relax together for a little while. How does that sound?"

"Just fine, Ma'am."

So he had that to look forward to as well.

***

Gemma Wentworth changed back into her britches and shirt, pulled on her boots. A dress wouldn't do for what came next.

It was too bad Clint Adams had to be killed. It would have been nice to spend some more time with him. She did have that sweet boy to use, but Clint Adams was a man. There was a big difference. Gately was sweet tasting, but Adams had that musky man smell and flavor to him. That was what she liked, and what she hadn't been getting from her husband for years. If only she could win Clint over to her side, but that didn't seem likely. So he and Roper were going to have to succumb to the superior force, and die.

The house had two bedrooms. One was hers, where she was now. She left that room, walked to the other, and entered. In the bed lay her husband. He had a wound from the war that had never healed correctly. Doctors said they couldn't do anything about it and said it would even eventually kill him. They seemed to be getting close to that. His time in Springfield seemed to have been his last burst of energy, but ever since they had traveled to Segundo he had been sickly and useless.

"Well, darling," she said, "how are we feeling to-day?"

He stared up at her from the bed, his eyes clouded by pain.

"If you'd get me a proper doctor—"

"You've had proper doctors, dear," she said. "They've all said the same thing."

"So you say," Wentworth said, "but you would like it if I died."

"Now," she said, "if that were true I could simply kill you while you lay there, helpless."

He actually chuckled, then grimaced with pain.

"Not your style, Gemma. You don't do your own killing."

"Perhaps not," she said, "but I have men who would do it for me."

Wentworth coughed and said, "Those are my men."

"Ah, but the sweet Captain Gately, he's all mine, dear," she said, smiling. "He'll do anything I want him to do."

"Whore!" he spat.

"Oh, he's got one of those," she said. "But I wanted you to know that the ransom money is here. We'll have it by the end of the day. All of it."

"For the last time, Gemma," he said. "Send to Trinidad for a proper doctor for me."

"Perhaps," she said. "We'll see, Samuel. Let's just wait and see."

THIRTY-EIGHT

nce again Clint and Roper rode into town. This time the streets were empty. The denizens of Segundo sensed that trouble was coming, and they had taken to their homes or closed up the doors and windows of their shops.

Clint and Roper saw Gately sitting in front of the hotel and rode up to him. His men came to attention, kept their eyes on the two men.

"You have the money?" Gately asked.

"Half, as we agreed."

Gately waved at Morehouse, who stepped into the street to peer into the saddlebags as Clint held them open. He started to reach in, but Clint said, "Un-uh," and closed the saddlebag.

Corporal Morehouse got back up onto the boardwalk and said to the Captain, "It's there."

"Very well." Gately got up from his chair. "Let's walk our friends over to their prize."

The Captain and his Corporal took the lead. Clint and Roper rode behind them, with the other men taking up the rear. Clint and Roper didn't like having those guns behind them, but didn't think the men would try anything until all the money was involved.

They followed Captain Gately toward the end of town, toward the Wentworth house, but did not go past the town line. Instead, they headed for a large livery stable that had two men in front of it. Wearing gray jackets, they were on guard.

"Open the doors," Gately said.

"Yes, sir."

The two men opened the double livery doors.

"Sir," one of them said, "the lady is inside."

"Good."

Gately turned to Clint and Roper. "You can dismount here."

They did. Clint untied his saddlebags and slung them over his shoulder. He knew if they wanted to take them away from him there was nothing he could do, but nobody made a move.

They followed Gately in, the other soldiers right behind them. Inside they saw a buckboard with a tarp thrown over the back. It was surrounded by soldiers—or rather, men in mended Confederate jackets—and standing right behind it, her arms folded, was Gemma Wentworth.

"Here is your precious President Lincoln," Gemma said.

"Uncover the casket."

Gemma waved and two men leaped up onto the buckboard and removed the tarp. The casket was a double to the one he had seen in the tomb.

"Do you want to open it?" Gemma asked.

Clint and Roper exchanged looks. After all these years would there be anything inside that could be recognizable?

"Can we be alone with it?" Clint asked.

"We can't do th—" Gately started, but Gemma cut him off, rolling her eyes.

"The stable will be surrounded. Let them be alone

170

with their precious President."

"Thank you," Clint said.

Gemma waved and all the solders moved to the front door. When they were outside they heard Gately order, "Surround the entire building!"

When the doors closed the interior was lit only by a few lamps.

"Why do we want to be alone with this?" Roper asked.

"I don't know," Clint said.

He climbed onto the back of the buckboard so he could examine the casket closely.

"It doesn't look like it's been open."

"Is it the right casket, or isn't it?" Roper asked.

"I don't know!" Clint said. "I haven't seen the real one in years. I did see a copy they put in its place so no one knows the real one's gone, and this looks just like that one."

"Looks like a Presidential casket," Roper said. "Lots of gold."

"These screws have not been tampered with."

"Why not?"

"What do you mean?"

"I mean if they hated him so much," Roper said, "why not tamper with the body?"

"I don't know," Clint said. "Maybe they're more concerned with the money."

"I think Mrs. Wentworth is," Roper said. "She's not so interested in helping the South to rise again."

"But these men are," Clint said. "How do you think they'd feel if they knew she wanted the money for herself?"

"They'd kill her."

Clint nodded.

"That the way you want to play it?"

"That might be the way we have to play it, to avoid a prolonged gun battle."

"These men... the ones who are trained are older, and the young ones probably haven't been trained."

"So you think we can handle them?"

"Under the right circumstances."

"We better figure out a way," Clint said, "to manipulate the circumstances."

THIRTY-NINE

lint and Roper opened the stable door. Gemma and Gately turned to face them, as did three men with guns.

"Okay," Clint said.

"You're satisfied?" Gemma asked.

"Yes."

"The money, then."

Clint turned his saddlebags upside down and dumped the money out onto the ground.

"I need my saddlebags."

Gemma said to Gately, "Have one of the men fetch a bag from inside."

Gately waved and one of them went in and came back with a burlap bag.

"Pick up the money," she said.

"Morehouse," Gately said.

The Corporal took the bag, went down on one knee, and put the money into the sack.

"Is that half?" she asked.

"Looks like it," Morehouse said.

"Is it or isn't it, Corporal?" Gately snapped.

"It is."

"Give it to me," Gemma said.

The solder handed over the bag.

"Hook a team up to the buckboard for them," she

said. "Ride out with them to get the rest of the money." She looked at Clint. "Once we have the rest of the money you can keep going."

"All right."

"Get some of the other men," Gately said to Morehouse. "Hook up a team."

"Yes, sir."

"I'll be at the house," Gemma said to Gately. "Let me know when it's over." She looked at Clint again. "Too bad we didn't have more time together."

"That's okay with me," Clint told her.

She stared at him, then nodded shortly, turned, and walked away. She presented a pretty picture walking away from them in pants. All the men paused to watch her, except the one who had gone inside to hook up the team.

"You and you, saddle horses for us," Gately told some of the remaining men. "The rest of you stay here and watch them."

"Yes, sir."

Gately looked at Clint and Roper.

"We'll be ready to move out shortly."

"You don't mind if we watch, do you?" Clint asked.

"No," Gately said, "that's fine."

Clint and Roper went in to watch the men hook up the team and to make sure there wasn't a switch of the casket.

*　*　*

When the buckboard was hooked to the team one of the soldiers drove it out of the livery. The casket was once again covered by a tarp. Clint looked underneath just to be sure.

"I can drive the buckboard," Roper offered. "That'll leave both of your hands empty. We can tie my horse to the back."

"Good idea." They both knew if there was gunplay Clint was the one who should have two hands free.

From around the corner they heard the sound of horses, and then six men with gray coats appeared.

"These men will accompany you," Gately said. "Corporal Morehouse will be in command."

"Can you trust them with fifty thousand dollars?" Clint asked.

"These men are loyal to the South," Gately said. "They can be trusted."

Clint looked at them. Morehouse looked old enough to have been in the war. Of the other six men, two might have been in the war as teens. The other four were too young--younger even than Captain Gately.

'Well," Clint said, loudly, "what do you say, gentlemen? Let's go get the rest of that money."

FORTY

Roper led the way, with a solder on either side of him. They had to stay to the main road because of the buckboard, which meant they wouldn't be able to drive right up to the hiding place where the money was. They were going to have to stop and have the men dismount rather than let them ride up to the place.

"Tal, why don't you stay with the body?" Clint suggested. "I'll take these men to the money."

"Fine with me."

"Stay with him," Morehouse said to two of the men.

"Yes, sir."

"The rest of you with me." Morehouse looked at Clint. "Lead the way."

Clint headed for the money, followed by five armed men. Roper was left behind with two armed men.

As Clint made his way to the rock hiding place he wondered how soon the men would make their move. There was no way they were going to let him and Roper leave with the body. What had worked in their favor was the fact that they hadn't had to manipulate the situation, at all. It was Gemma, and Gately, who had made the mistake of sending only seven men with them—unless there were more minutes behind them.

Whatever happened would have to happen fast, before other forces could arrive.

"Come on, Adams," Morehouse said, "stop stallin'."

"I'm not stalling," Clint said. "I'm trying to remember—"

"You were just here," Morehouse said. "You're stallin'."

"Wait," Clint said, "I think it's there—yes, there," he pointed, "that pile of rocks."

"Dig it out," Morehouse said to two of his men.

Clint stood back and got ready. As soon as they saw the money they were sure to turn their guns on him. He knew Gemma was counting on that, and she won either way it went.

The men tossed the rocks away, uncovered the opening, reached in, and came out with the saddlebags.

"Come on, come on," Morehouse said, "look inside."

The men did, and one of them said, "It's full of money."

The other man started to reach for his gun, and Clint could hear the other men bringing their rifles to bear, but as he went to draw his own gun Morehouse called out, "Wait, hold it!"

Everyone stopped.

"Adams, they want us to kill you and your friend," the Corporal said. "As soon as they hear shots here my other men are to kill Roper."

"Why are you telling me something I already know?"

"Because I—you know?"

"Of course," Clint said. "Gemma Wentworth is not about to let us ride away alive."

"Well, I'll let you ride away alive," Morehouse said. "My men and I will take the money, and we'll go our separate ways. What do you say?"

"I say no."

"You didn't even think about it!"

178

"I don't have to," Clint said. "I'm not letting Gemma, or your Captain, get away with anything."

"So go back to town and get the other half of the money from them. They've got a force of about fourteen left there without us. Just let us go with this money."

"I can't do that, Morehouse," Clint said, "but I tell you what I will do. You boys know who I am. I think I can take the five of you. If not, I'll kill three, maybe four. But I'll let you all go if you'll leave the money behind."

"Leave the money?" Morehouse asked.

"That's right."

"I can't do that," Morehouse said.

"I can," one man said, raising his hand. "I don't wanna go against you, Mr. Adams. If you'll let me walk away, I will."

"Anybody else?" Clint asked.

"You can't—" Morehouse started.

"Yeah," another man said—actually more of a boy, "me. This has all got out of hand, and that woman is crazy."

"You've got that right, son," Clint said. "You two drop your guns."

They did.

"Now just stand aside. If you go back to the wagon now Mr. Roper might kill you by accident. When this is over I'll take you down to your horses."

The two men raised their hands and stepped away from their guns. They were the two men who had dug out the money, but apparently even the sight of it wasn't enough to make them risk their lives.

"Now it's the three of you," Clint said.

"Fifty thousand, men," Morehouse said, "and now it's a bigger split without them." He indicated the two men who had dropped their weapons.

The other two soldiers exchanged a glance, then looked at Morehouse.

"We already got our rifles in our hands," one of them said.

"Yeah, you do," Clint said, "which means I'll have to kill the two of you first."

"He's bluffing!" Morehouse said.

"Your call," Clint said.

But at that moment the call was made for all of them. There were some shots from back where they'd left the wagon and Clint went ahead and made his move.

He drew his gun, surprising both of the men who were holding their rifles. He shot them both dead, then turned his gun to Morehouse, who was only just clearing his holster.

"Wait, wait—" he pleaded, but it was too late. Clint shot him once, right in the center of the chest. Morehouse's eyes went wide and he fell over backwards.

"Jesus Christ!" one of the other men said.

"Grab those saddlebags and come on!" Clint said. He started running toward the wagon.

FORTY-ONE

Killing the two soldiers was not Roper's choice.

He and the two men watched as Clint took the other five men to retrieve the money. Roper could see that the two young men were nervous. He didn't know whose decision it was to send all young men with them to fetch the money, but because they had no experience they were extremely jumpy.

"Take it easy, boys," Roper said. "They'll be back."

"You shut up!" one of them said. They were both holding rifles pointed at Roper, who thought he might get shot by accident.

"Okay, okay," Roper said, "I'm not saying a word." But he kept his hand down by his gun. What kind of a senseless death would it be to be shot by accident by two nervous boys?

But when Clint and the others didn't come back right away the two boys became even more nervous, for a different reason.

"What if they take off with the money?" one of them asked the other. "We don't get our share."

That was when Roper knew these men had no intention of returning to town with the money.

"We got their horses," the second man said.

"They can buy new horses with fifty thousand dollars!" the first one said.

"So whataya wanna do?"

"We gotta do somethin' before they get away!"

They both looked at Roper and he knew what was coming. He didn't wait. He drew his gun even as they tightened their fingers on the triggers. He fired once, threw himself into the bed of the buckboard with the casket, and then fired two more times.

Both young would-be Confederate soldiers lay dead on the ground.

***

Clint came running up to the wagon, but stopped when he saw Roper standing by the casket.

"What happened?" he asked.

"They got nervous. You?"

The other two soldiers came running up behind him and Roper started to go for his gun.

"No!" Clint yelled. "They dropped their guns and surrendered."

"And the others?"

"Not so lucky." Clint turned to the two men. "Toss him the saddlebags."

The man holding them obeyed, tossing them up to Roper.

Clint walked around the wagon, saw the two men lying on the ground.

"They weren't so lucky, either," Roper said.

"I can see that."

"What about these two?" Roper asked.

"They're free to go," Clint said. He looked at them. "Take off those jackets, mount up, and go."

"Yessir!" they both said.

They stripped off their jackets and left them lying

in the dirt as they mounted up and rode off, away from town.

"What are we facing back in town?" Roper asked.

"About fourteen men," Clint said.

"Could be worse," Roper said. "Of course, we have half the ransom and the casket. We could just go."

"Yeah, we could."

They stared at each other for a few minutes.

"You can't do that, can you?" Roper asked.

"No," Clint said. "Can you?"

Roper backed off answering and said, "It's your call."

Clint looked at the two dead men, and then the five horses that belonged to all the dead soldiers.

"We better tie these horses off so they don't go back to town and tip them off."

"I think when these fellas, and those others you killed, don't return with the money, that'll pretty much tip them off."

"Which is why we can't wait," Clint said. "We have to move fast."

"So, back to town."

Clint nodded.

"And what do we do with the casket? And the money?"

"We'll take the money with us," Clint said. "We'll have to leave the buckboard and casket out here somewhere."

"But where?"

"Well," Clint said, "off the main road, for sure."

"Okay," Roper said. "We've got to hide the buckboard, the casket, and five horses. That shouldn't be too hard."

Clint gathered up the five horses, tied them to the back of the buckboard, then mounted Eclipse.

"Let's go," he said, "Maybe all we have to do is get far enough off the road."

***

As it happened, they found a clearing inside a ring of trees and rocks where the wagon could sit out of sight. They formed a picket line for the horses, and as long as they remained quiet they'd stay hidden, as well.

"I hate to leave the President here," Clint said, putting his hand on the casket.

"If he's even in there," Roper said.

"He's in there," Clint said, then added, "we have to believe he's in there."

"Yeah, okay," Roper said, "he's in there. And he'll still be here when we get back." After a moment Roper added, "If we get back."

"Check your guns," Clint said. They made sure their pistols and rifles were in proper working order, then mounted up.

"Where to first?" Roper asked.

"Let's circle around and see if we can catch Gemma in her house," Clint said. "We might be able to use her as a hostage and get the other men to disarm."

"I'm a little worried about this young Captain Gately," Roper said.

"What about him?"

"He was too young to be in the war. I think he might be looking for a way to prove himself."

"Given the chance, then, he might make the wrong decision," Clint said. "I think what we're going to have to do is take that decision away from him."

FORTY-TWO

It was getting on toward dusk as Clint and Roper came within sight of the Wentworth house. The townspeople still had not returned to the streets. Clint didn't know how many of them there were, or how long Gately and his men had been in Segundo. But without law nobody would go against them, and he doubted Sheriff Harlan from Trinidad would want to risk his life for Segundo.

"We better leave the horses here," Clint said.

"She's got to have guards," Roper said, as they dismounted.

"I'll circle around and we'll come at the house from different sides."

"How do we know where the money is?"

"I know," Clint said. "She's got the money. She wouldn't trust it to anyone else."

"All right. How long?"

"Count to sixty and then move in. I'll be in position by then."

"I'll take the front."

"Okay," Clint said, "I'll go in the back."

Roper hunkered down as Clint moved to circle to the front of the house.

In fifty-eight seconds he was in position...

***

185

Gately looked at Gemma Wentworth, lying naked on her bed. For a woman in her forties she had a lovely body, full breasts and hips, smooth skin, and an appetite for sex of a much younger woman—like his whore, Katy.

He was naked as well, standing by her bed. She was stroking his cock with one hand, murmuring to him.

"Pretty," she said, "such a pretty thing and so sweet... come on... come to bed..."

He knew her husband was in the next room, but it didn't matter. While his penis was so hard it didn't matter, and while there was the money it didn't matter. Together they would use the money to build a new South.

"Quickly," she said, "they'll be back soon, with the rest of the money... quickly..."

He joined her on the bed, lowered himself onto her, and slid into her steamy depths, which closed around him like a wet fist...

***

Clint moved in on the house, saw the soldier standing by the front door. He was one of the young ones. It was no trouble to sneak up on him and render him unconscious. He lowered him to the ground easily. He didn't have anything to tie him with, but decided not to kill him. Maybe it would be all over before he woke. He took his pistol and rifle and tossed them as far as he could, then moved to the front door. . .

***

At the same time, Roper moved in on the guard at the back of the house. Just one man in front, and one in back. He wondered if that meant there were more inside?

This was one of the older soldiers, who had put in his

J.R. ROBERTS

time during the war. He was trained, and started to turn as Roper got closer, but it was too late. Roper hit him over the head with the butt of his gun—something he hated to do because it could damage the weapon—and lowered the man to the ground. He took his guns and tossed them, moved to the back door, which was not locked, and opened it...

***

The front door was locked, but Clint was able to force it without much fuss or noise. When he was inside he moved quietly, stopped in the empty living room, and listened. He heard the unmistakable sounds of two people having sex, and started to follow it when the kitchen door opened and Roper stepped through.

"Simon was in the kitchen," Roper said. "I used some towels to tie him."

"Good."

"Sounds like someone's busy," Roper said.

"Let's go see who it is."

FORTY-THREE

oth men moved toward the sound, down a hall. They came to another bedroom first, where a man was lying in bed.

"Wait," Clint said. He stepped inside, moved to the bed and looked down at Samuel Wentworth. He touched the Colonel, then went back to the hall.

"Dead?" Roper asked.

Clint nodded. "Must have died within the last hour."

They continued down the hall toward the sound of a squeaking bed and two people grunting. Clint recognized the sounds Gemma made during sex. When they got to the door they paused and watched as Captain Gately's bare ass moved up and down, up and down, with Gemma's shapely legs wrapped around his waist.

"Should we wait for them to finish?" Roper whispered.

"No," Clint said aloud, and then even louder, "Sorry to barge in, folks!"

Gately rolled off of Gemma quickly and stared at them with wide eyes. His gun was not within easy reach as he looked around. It was on a chair across the room.

"Go ahead," Clint said. "Try for it."

"Relax, Captain," Gemma said, looking at Clint with no hint of surprise. "Just get your pants on. They won't shoot you for doing that."

"No," Roper said, "I think I like him just the way he is."

"Do you mind if I get up, then?" Gemma asked.

"No," Clint said, "I think you should both stay right where you are."

Gemma moved her hips and said, "Well, he's gone quite soft now."

"Not my problem," Clint said. "Where's the money, Gemma?"

"I knew you'd come back," she said.

"I'll have a look around," Roper said, and started to search the room.

"What—what did you do to my men?" Gately asked.

"They're dead or gone," Clint said. "Not coming back. And the men you left outside are down. So with you here that leaves... what? Eleven more?"

"Eleven is enough," Gemma said. "You don't have a chance."

"Against eleven trained men, maybe not," Clint said, "but this ragtag group? Don't make me laugh, Gemma."

"Please," Gately said, "can I get up and at least put my pants on?"

"Feeling vulnerable, Captain?" Roper asked. To Clint he said, "I'll search the rest of the house."

Gemma moved uncomfortably beneath Gately, whose arms were obviously getting tired.

"Can I sit up?" he asked.

"No, just stay where you are. I like you both this way."

"This is ridiculous," Gemma said. "I'm sorry you found me like this, Clint, but you know you came back for me."

"Did I?"

"Me and the money," she said.

"You're half right."

"Oh, don't bruise my ego and tell me it's the money."

"Got it!" Clint heard Roper shout. In moments he appeared at the door, holding the saddlebags.

"She put them in her husband's room."

"Who'd look there?" she asked.

"You know he's dead, don't you?" Clint asked.

"The man I married died a long time ago," she said. "Look, eleven men is eleven men, trained or not. By sheer force of numbers you can't make it."

"We can ride out without them ever knowing we were here," Clint said. "By the time you tell them we'll be long gone."

"I'll send them after you," she said. "If you're going to take the money why not take me, too?"

"Ma'am?" Gately said, staring down at her. "What about the cause?"

"Oh, grow up, Captain," she said. "A hundred thousand dollars buys lots of causes."

"But . . the South—"

"—died a long time ago. Time to stop playing soldier, Edward."

"Playing?"

"That's what you've been doing, you know," she said. "Playing. You, my husband, the rest of those misfits. Oh, get off me, he's not going to shoot you!"

She pushed him off her, got to her feet, reached for a robe, and covered her naked body.

Gately sat there on the bed, waiting to be shot, or just too stunned to move. Clint figured he had plans of his own, maybe for Gemma, maybe for the cause, but now he was realizing he had nothing.

"Sorry, Captain," Roper said. He crossed the room and clubbed the man over the head with his gun, figuring he might have to buy a new one after this.

"Ooh," Gemma said, making a pained face, "was that really necessary?"

"I'm afraid so," Clint said, while Roper used the sheets to truss the Captain up.

"He's going to be terribly embarrassed and angry when he wakes up," she said. "And those men might follow him. You really do have to take me with you, you know. They might kill me... or worse."

"That's true," Clint said.

Roper finished with Gately and looked at Clint.

"Tie her up, too," Clint said.

"Clint!"

Roper grabbed her, getting a strong whiff of sex, tore some sheets and used them to tie her hands and feet.

"You can't," she said, looking concerned for the first time. "This isn't funny, darling."

"Actually," Clint said, "it is kind of funny. What do you think, Tal?"

Roper joined him at the door and said, "Looks pretty funny, to me."

"You better gag her," Clint said. "She might yell, and if she has time to talk to the others before he does, she might get them on her side. After all, she's a very persuasive woman."

"Gotcha."

"Clint, don't—" she said, but Roper cut her off by stuffing some strips of sheet into her mouth, and then tying one around her head.

"Sorry, Gemma," Clint said. "Time for us to go."

They hurried down the hall to the back door and out. Roper noticed that the man he'd knocked out was gone and said to Clint, "Hey, wait—" but before he could speak any further men with guns appeared from around the corner.

"Shit," Clint said.

FORTY-FOUR

"What's goin' on?" one of them demanded.

"That's the one who hit me," one of them said, pointing at Roper.

Before long they found themselves facing about eight men. The others must have been in front of the house, or in a saloon or cathouse—or maybe the count they had been given was high.

"The Colonel's inside, dead," Clint said. "He died in his bed. We found your Captain in bed with his wife."

"So what?" another solder said. "She looks like she needs it every day. Maybe tomorrow it'll be one of us." He laughed at his own comment.

"I don't think so," Clint said. "See, Mrs. Wentworth was going to take the money and leave..." then he had a thought and added, "... and take the young Captain with her."

"What?" someone said.

"They wuz gonna leave us?"

"What about the cause?" one young man asked.

An older man said, "Don't be daft, sonny. There ain't no cause. There's only the money. That's all there ever was."

Another man pointed to the saddlebags on Clint's shoulder.

"Is that it? Is that the money?"

"Half of it," Clint said.

"Where's the other half?" someone asked.

"Hidden."

"Well," the older man said, "you better unhide it right quick. We'll all take our shares and light out, and you can stay alive."

"What about the lady and her Captain?" Roper asked. "They're tied up inside."

"Hell, leave 'em there," the older man said.

"B-but, the South—" the younger man said.

"Will you shut up about that!" the older man said. "There ain't no South." To illustrate his point he took off his jacket and tossed it to the ground. "See these jackets they gave us. Torn and mended? I think that there might be the same one I was wearin' the day Lee surrendered."

Other men followed, and soon their jackets were all on the ground, including the idealistic young man, who was still frowning, confused.

"And those guns?" Clint asked. "Some of them look pretty old. Have you drilled with them? Are you sure they work?"

"Don't you worry about our guns," the older man said. "They work, all right."

"Well, yours might," Clint said. "You strike me as the kind of man who takes care of his weapon, but what about the rest of these men? That kid, there. I don't think he knows the first thing about caring for a weapon."

Roper shifted uncomfortably. He was willing to let Clint do all the talking, but he knew eventually they were going to have to go into action.

"Look," the older man said, "drop the saddlebags, show us where the rest of the money is, and you can go. If not, then you're gonna find out if our guns work."

"I don't think so," Clint said,

"Whataya mean?" the man asked.

"I don't think I'll drop the saddlebags. Or show you where the rest of the money is," Clint said. "What do you think, Tal?"

"I think," Roper said, "that we should all find out together whether their guns work or not."

"There you go," Clint said. "Your call, gents."

The older man studied Clint for a few moments. The other men obviously looked to him for guidance, and he knew it.

"Come on, now," he said. "There are only two of you."

"Two's plenty," Clint said, "when you know what you're doing."

"You guys are crazy," the man said.

"What's your name?" Clint asked.

"George Parish."

"George," Roper said, "do you know who he is?" He pointed at Clint.

"Yeah, yeah," George said, "he's the Gunsmith, we wuz all told that."

"So you better be sure your guns are in proper working order," Roper said, "because it's the only chance you've got."

The other men looked toward Parish. Clint and Roper knew it was up to one man what happened in the next few moments.

"And money's money," Parish said, and went for his gun.

Damn! Clint thought.

FORTY-FIVE

Since they looked to Parish for direction, Clint had to take him first. He outdrew the man cleanly and shot him in the chest.

Roper drew, shot the man directly behind Parish.

Two of the would-be soldiers brought their rifles to bear, but as Clint had suspected, the weapons misfired.

Two other men drew their pistols, but before they could employ them Clint shot one and Roper shot the other.

In seconds, four men were on the ground, and four others were struggling with their weapons.

"Just drop 'em, gents," Clint said. "They're not going to work."

The four men—all young—looked at Clint and Roper and dropped their useless guns to the ground.

"D-don't shoot," one of them said, and they all raised their hands.

"You boys all have to find new lives," Clint said. "The people inside the house don't have your best interests at heart."

"It's up to you if you want to untie them, after we leave," Roper said.

"Or whatever you want to do with them," Clint said, "just don't let them talk you into coming after us."

"W-we won't," one of them said.

"Good," Roper said. "Now move aside."

Clint and Roper hurried to their horses, relieved to find them—and the saddlebags with the other fifty thousand dollars—still there. As they rode away they saw three men in gray jackets running toward them. They came up short when they saw the two men on horses, hands grabbing for their guns.

"Hold it!" Clint said, drawing his gun and pointing it, something he rarely did. Usually when he drew, he fired, but these were also young men.

"W-what's happenin'?" one of them asked.

"It's all over," Clint said.

"What is?"

"The South has fallen..." Clint said.

"...again," Roper added.

The three men looked past them at the Wentworth house.

"Some of your comrades are still alive," Clint said. "They'll explain everything to you. Drop your guns to the ground and go and find out."

They obeyed and moved past the two mounted men warily. Clint and Roper turned and watched the three men run toward the house.

"What do you think?" Roper asked.

"I think we were right," Clint said. "The South *has* fallen..."

"... again!" Roper said.

FORTY-SIX

When the train pulled into Springfield, Illinois, Jeremy Pike was waiting. Clint stepped off and shook hands with the men.

"Did you find Wentworth?" Pike asked.

"You know about Wentworth?"

"I talked with Detective Kingman," Pike said. "He told me a lot, I told him very little."

"Dead," Clint said. "What about Wyatt?"

"Dead," Pike said. "Wentworth must have killed him before he left town."

Clint didn't tell the man it was probably Gemma Wentworth who had killed the big man—maybe after showing him some intense pleasure first. That seemed to be her way.

"I assume you have transportation?" Clint asked.

"Yes," Pike said. "There's a hearse waiting outside."

"A hearse. Isn't that obvious?"

"Nobody will know it's Lincoln inside," Pike said. "Just some poor soul on his way to his final resting place."

"Won't they wonder about the guards?"

"No guards," Pike said. "Just me."

"And me?"

"Not necessary," Pike said. "Your job is done, Clint. You can get back on this train and continue on, or take the next one going the other way. Or you can mount up and ride out. That's up to you. Washington thanks you for your service."

The two men shook hands again.

"I'm also authorized to pay you—"

"That reminds me," Clint said. "I redeposited the hundred thousand into the bank." To do that they had avoided Trinidad, not wanting to deal with would-be thieves there, and waited until they had reached Colorado Springs.

"We know, we saw that. They didn't really expect you to get the body back and keep the money. It was a nice surprise. I'm authorized to offer you ten percent."

"As much as I'd like to take it," Clint said, "I can't. Not for bringing the President back."

"I understand," Pike said. "You knew him."

"I did," Clint said, "so it was important for me to bring him back."

"I'm sure if the family—and the country—knew what you did, they'd be grateful."

"On the other hand," Clint said, "I couldn't have done it without Talbot Roper's help, so..."

"I'll see that the ten per cent is sent to him," Pike said.

"Thank you."

"And now I must see to offloading the casket," Pike said. "Until we meet again, my friend."

They shook hands. Pike went to see to the casket, while Clint went to get Eclipse from the stock car. He intended to mount up and ride out, but first he needed to make amends with a certain hotel owner's daughter.

The End

ABOUT THE AUTHOR

As "J.R. Roberts" Bob Randisi is the creator and author of the long running western series, *The Gunsmith*. Under various other pseudonyms he has created and written the "Tracker," "Mountain Jack Pike," "Angel Eyes," "Ryder," "Talbot Roper," "The Son of Daniel Shaye," and "the Gamblers" Western series. His western short story collection, *The Cast-Iron Star and Other Western Stories*, is now available in print and as an ebook from Western Fictioneers Books.

In the mystery genre he is the author of the *Miles Jacoby, Nick Delvecchio, Gil & Claire Hunt, Dennis McQueen, Joe Keough*, and *The Rat Pack*, series. He has written more than 500 western novels and has worked in the Western, Mystery, Sci-Fi, Horror and Spy genres. He is the editor of over 30 anthologies. All told he is the author of over 650 novels. His arms are very, very tired.

He is the founder of the Private Eye Writers of America, the creator of the Shamus Award, the co-founder of Mystery Scene Magazine, the American Crime Writers League, Western Fictioneers and their Peacemaker Award.

In 2009 the Private Eye Writers of America awarded him the Life Achievement Award, and in 2013 the Readwest Foundation presented him with their President's Award for Life Achievement.